D1575279

Over the River

Over the River

SHARELLE BYARS
MORANVILLE

HENRY HOLT AND COMPANY

NEW YORK

Henry Holt and Company, LLC
Publishers since 1866
115 West 18th Street, New York, New York 10011
www.henryholt.com

Henry Holt is a registered trademark of Henry Holt and Company, LLC
Copyright © 2002 by Sharelle Byars Moranville
All rights reserved.
Distributed in Canada by H. B. Fenn and Company Ltd.

Library of Congress Cataloging-in-Publication Data
Moranville, Sharelle Byars. Over the river / Sharelle Byars Moranville.
p.   cm.
Summary: In 1947, after the war, Willa Mae's father returns to the Illinois town where
she has lived with her maternal grandparents for the last five of her eleven years, and
Willa Mae finds herself struggling to understand old family tensions and secrets.
[1. Family problems—Fiction.   2. Farm life—Illinois—Fiction.   3. Fathers
and daughters—Fiction.   4. Grandparents—Fiction.   5. Secrets—Fiction.
6. Illinois—History—20th century—Fiction.]   I. Title.
PZ7.M78825 Ov 2002   [Fic]—dc21   2002024308

ISBN 0-8050-7049-4 / First Edition—2002 / Designed by Donna Mark
Printed in the United States of America on acid-free paper. ∞

1 3 5 7 9 10 8 6 4 2

To my mother, Alma Byars,
who wrote and kept the letters, and
to my editor, Christy Ottaviano,
who read and nurtured the story

—S. B. M.

Over the River

Chapter 1

"I see the angel's wings," I called out, but Nana and Aunty Rose didn't answer.

They were puffing from carrying the sloshing washtub full of peonies and lilacs. I hugged an armful of empty quart jars against my chest.

As we walked up the hill, Mama's angel showed more and more of herself, rising up against the blue Memorial Day sky.

Panther Fork was turned out to decorate graves.

Wren Roberts, small and neat as the bird she got her name from, stood up from Lonnie Dale's grave, brushing dirt off her hands.

"That's a fine bunch of lilacs you've got there, Mae," she said to Nana.

Nana motioned Aunty Rose to set down the washtub.

"They grow on the south side," Nana observed, flexing her hand. "Don't Lonnie Dale's grave look nice?"

Wren turned to where Nana was looking. Lonnie Dale's monument, a column of gray granite carved like the stump of a tree, was ringed with red and yellow tulips.

"Seems like yesterday he was pestering me about this and that," Wren said, her mouth twisting.

Two years ago, Lonnie Dale Roberts got killed by a piano. He was helping his daddy move it into the back of a pickup when the rope broke, and the piano rolled out of the truck bed and mashed Lonnie Dale right into the ground.

Lonnie Dale had been only fourteen, and folks couldn't seem to get over the fact that one so young had died in such a bad way. Getting killed by a piano seemed worse than dying of appendicitis or even getting struck by lightning.

"Well, I guess it's part of living." Wren shook her head. "We all got folks here." And she looked up the hill at Mama's angel, which was far and away the grandest monument in the cemetery.

I never thought of Mama when I looked at the angel. I thought of God Himself, grand and pure and white.

Nana and Wren nodded at the sureness of death, then Nana and Aunty Rose picked up the washtub again, and I led the way on up the hill.

Water slopped out of the tub, turning Nana's canvas shoes dark, as she and Aunty Rose lowered the flowers by Mama's grave.

"Careful," Nana said to Aunty Rose. "Don't slop. It's all the water we got. You can just set the mason jars down over there, Willa Mae," she said to me, pointing to a spot off to the side where the spring grass grew in thick clumps.

"I want to walk around," Aunty Rose said, her feet, in neatly polished saddle oxfords, practically dancing. She smoothed the front of her new blue weskit and practiced her dimples right there in broad daylight before she looked over and waved at Joe Keifer.

Poor Joe Keifer. He would get his hopes up, only to find Aunty Rose could flirt with a garden hoe.

Nana shook her head, trying not to smile. But it was hard, because Aunty Rose just naturally made people smile.

"Walk around and look at the graves," Nana told her. "Go see if Retus's family has decorated the folks' grave yet."

The *folks* were Grandpa's parents, Great-grandma and Great-grandpa Shannon, and Retus was Grandpa's oldest brother.

"Willa Mae and I'll fix the flowers here," Nana said, dropping to her knees at the base of Mama's monument.

Aunty Rose went off, and Nana began dunking the empty mason jars in water.

"Want to fix the lilacs?" she asked me, handing me a jar.

I took the big wobbly stems of lilacs out of the washtub and arranged them in the jars, brushing away a bee that kept pestering.

"You ought to pull the leaves off that go under the water," Nana said, watching me. "The flowers will stay nicer that way."

She took each of the jars and settled them into the dirt that she had loosened with her trowel.

After a while, I put my hands to my shoulders. "Feel the sun, Nana," I said.

Nana's hand was cool, the calluses nicely rough, like a kitten's tongue. "You should have worn a sun hat," she said.

Nana's broad-brimmed straw hat, tied under her chin, threw her face and shoulders into shadow.

"Aunty Rose didn't wear one," I said. "She told me it made her look like a fat China woman."

"If Rose jumped in the lake, would you jump too?"

"Maybe," I said. Aunty Rose was sixteen and knew about things.

Nana dipped her hands in the water and patted my shoulders, letting the cool water trickle down my arms.

"We're about done," she said. "Just let me finish settling the peonies in."

Mama's angel was standing on a cloud of pink and purple flowers, her marble toes, straight and cool, barely touching the blossoms. She seemed like she was about to ascend straight to heaven with Jesus and Elijah.

"Hey, Willa Mae."

The voice came from over by the big thorny locust, where Petey Tyler and his brother Thomas were poking a stick at something in the weeds.

Petey motioned to me.

Petey Tyler had freckles and thin lips that curved halfway back to his ears. He couldn't help it, but he looked like a frog. Aunty Rose said he just needed to find the right girl to kiss him and he'd turn into a prince. For Petey's sake, I hoped he found the right girl soon.

I bet the boys had a terrapin. I waved back, but I didn't go over. It didn't seem respectful by my very own mama's grave to go tearing off to play with a terrapin while Nana was still arranging the flowers.

I ran my fingers along the grooves cut into the base of the marble angel.

TREVA LORRAINE CLARK
MARCH 11, 1917–NOVEMBER 25, 1941
DEARLY LOVED

Mama? I said, and waited, listening hard.

After a while, I decided the only thing I heard was a plane droning, a bunch of birds, and people talking.

Mama almost never answered anymore. She'd gone on to busy herself with heavenly stuff, figuring I was eleven years old now, almost twelve, and in Grandpa's and Nana's good hands.

Aunty Rose waved from the low sandstone fence that outlined the cemetery. She was sitting there, swinging her legs, her bobby socks white as the angel's wings in the sunlight, her arm touching Joe's, who looked like he'd been set afire.

"There," Nana said, standing up and stepping back to look. "Don't that look nice."

"Yes, ma'am," I said, noticing that Nana never really looked at the angel. I don't think she thought about Mama when we decorated the grave, either. I think she saved those thoughts for times when she was alone and could let her face twist up the way I'd found her one day when I caught her looking through a box of old pictures.

The washtub without the water was light, and we carried it back to the road where Aunty Rose had parked. Cars lined the grassy ditch.

Everybody we met coming into the cemetery said, "Morning, Mae. Morning, Willa Mae." If Grandpa hadn't had to stay home and work on the disc, they'd have said, "Morning, Will. Morning, Mae. Morning, Willa Mae."

Having Grandpa's and Nana's names was like being hugged by two arms every time somebody spoke to me.

People were starting to forget that my mama had died six years ago and that I had a daddy who never did come home from the navy—and here the war was over for two whole years. People mainly remembered that I belonged to Will and Mae Shannon.

We put the washtub in the trunk of the old Packard and walked back to the cemetery.

The small military flags on the servicemen's graves snapped in the breeze, and Mama's angel seemed to preside over the whole Memorial Day doings.

Nana hugged me to her, then patted me on the rear end.

"I aim to walk around," she said. "You can come along, or you can be with the kids. Whatever you want."

I didn't care a thing about the terrapin, and I knew Aunty Rose might tease me about kissing a frog if I got too close to Petey Tyler, so I tagged along after Nana.

Uncle Retus's family had made Great-grandma and Great-grandpa Shannon's grave look real nice with a grapevine wreath and some daisies and lilies of the valley woven into it.

"It won't last past noon," Nana said, "the flowers not being in water." Then I guess she remembered what she was always telling me about how if you can't say something nice, don't say anything, because she added, "It sure looks pretty now, though."

The Millers, the whole lot of them, the nine kids stairstepped from Mike, who was Aunty Rose's age, to the baby in his mama's arms, were visiting Mr. Miller's grave, all sunk in from the casket still settling. Last Valentine's

Day, when he was in the barn milking, something had ruptured in Mr. Miller's head and he had bled to death inside.

Mrs. Miller had gotten a job with the telephone company in Huxley last month, which folks said was scandalous, leaving all those little ones at home to look after each other. But Mrs. Miller said if they weren't going to end up in the poorhouse, she had to work to put food on the table.

"Morning, Moira," Nana said. Then she spoke to each of the kids in turn, naming them off as if they were our own kin.

Nana knew their names and ages and sizes and was putting together a box of nice used clothing for the family.

"People don't like to take charity," she'd said to me last week as she folded some sweaters that would fit the two girls who were about my age. "But a family of ten can't live on telephone company wages. And ain't anybody likely to marry a widow with nine youngsters. Not even if she is still pretty."

Mrs. Miller held the baby over her shoulder, patting him. Little Mickey was bald as an onion and wore a white bonnet to keep off the sun.

One of the older Miller boys was turning up the earth

for a rosebush that lay beside the small, square marker with Mr. Miller's name and dates.

"We dug the rose up from the home place," Mrs. Miller said to Nana and me. "We thought Matthew would like that."

Since the funeral, Mrs. Miller's hair had gone from a pretty chestnut color to snow white.

"Do you want to walk around?" I asked Marilee and Mattie. Marilee was in my grade at school, and Mattie was a year behind. "Until your mama's ready?"

Mrs. Miller nodded that it was okay, and we took off.

"Let's go see Lizzie Mason's grave," I said.

We ran as fast as it was acceptable to run in a cemetery to the small white pillar under the cedar tree. Clear back in 1902, Lizzie Mason had eaten green apples one evening and been dead before morning. After Nana told me that story, I'd been very careful. I ate peaches, cherries, and even gooseberries—sour as they were—rather than take a chance on apples.

"I like the grave of the girl who died of hydrophobia better," Marilee said after we'd stood around Lizzie Mason's tilting monument for a while, acting solemn.

"Where is it?" I asked, giving Marilee and Mattie a

chance to show me something, though everybody knew the story of Nora Gently and the mad dog.

Marilee and Mattie led me over the hill, past Mama's angel and the old thorn tree where the Tyler boys had found the terrapin earlier. At the edge of the cemetery, the little grave was covered with snowy blossoms from the crab apple tree that shaded it.

"Nora Gently," Marilee read, though the letters were so worn, you had to know what they said. "Born 1897, died 1907."

"A mad dog chased her," Mattie said, telling the story as if anybody living in Billings Township hadn't already heard it a hundred times. "And his teeth caught her skirt, then she ran in the house and slammed the door. Later her daddy shot the dog, but that night when Nora Gently was mending her torn skirt, she bit off the thread that she had sewed with."

"And," Marilee said, "she got the hydrophobia from the thread that went through the skirt material the mad dog had slobbered on."

"And the next thing they knew," Mattie said, "she took sick and started foaming at the mouth, then she went insane and died."

I shivered. When I thought about dying, I didn't much want to do it. Mainly because it would grieve Nana and Grandpa and Aunty Rose. But I didn't want them to die and leave me, either. That would be a whole lot worse. I often put my head in Nana's lap and prayed that we could all just go together when the time came.

Marilee, Mattie, and I were still standing there at Nora Gently's grave when my other grandmother, Grandmother Clark, came over. I just looked up and there she was, holding a big basket of flowers.

"Who's this pretty girl?" she said, smiling at me.

When she set the basket down and reached out to put her hand on my head, I didn't know what to do. Then I remembered that Grandpa had stayed home to repair the harrow, so I could talk to Grandmother Clark without starting up World War II all over again.

"Hello, Grandmother Clark," I said. "Nice day for decorating the cemetery."

"It surely is," she said. "I'm just going over to put these flowers on my parents' grave."

I hadn't talked to Grandmother Clark since back in the winter, when Aunty Rose and I saw her at Lorrimer's General Store.

"We don't see enough of you. Are your folks doing well?"

"Yes, ma'am," I answered. "Nana's here. And Aunty Rose. Grandpa stayed home."

Her shoulders relaxed a little at the news Grandpa wasn't around.

"I've got a letter that might interest you," she said. "I've got it right here in my pocketbook. It's from your daddy."

She snapped open her black purse.

"Would you like to hear some of it?" she asked.

I nodded but wondered why I'd never gotten a letter from him myself. I guess he didn't think much about me—which was okay because I didn't think much about him anymore, either.

Grandmother Clark rustled through the pages until nearly the end. "This is the part for you," she said, adjusting her glasses. "'If you happen to see Mae Bug,'" she read, "'tell her I've been thinking about her extra hard. Sometimes I get mighty tired of this man's navy.'"

"Wouldn't it be fine if Harold came home?" Grandmother Clark asked, her eyes shining.

"Yes, ma'am," I said, just to be polite. "I bet you'd be glad to see him."

The light in Grandmother Clark's expression wavered as she put the letter away.

"Will you ask Will and Mae if you can come down and visit us someday?" she said. "We'd like that."

I swallowed. I wouldn't dare ask Grandpa if I could go visit the Clarks. But I hated to hurt Grandmother Clark's feelings.

"That would be nice," I said. "We'll have to see."

We'll have to see. That was what Nana said when something wasn't going to happen, but she didn't want to fuss about it.

"Well, you girls enjoy your day," Grandmother Clark said, suddenly including Marilee and Mattie in her conversation. "Willa Mae, it was sure good talking to you."

When Grandmother Clark had passed out of earshot, Marilee whispered, "I didn't know you had a daddy. Where's he been all this time?"

"In the navy. Fighting for his country," I said, not wanting her to think bad of him for some reason. "I expect he'll be home soon now they can spare him."

"So will you live with him?" Mattie asked.

"Of course not," I said.

I saw Nana coming toward us. She was stepping along like she was ready to go home. I wondered if she'd seen me talking to Grandmother Clark.

"Your mama needs you, girls," she said to Marilee and Mattie.

"Bye, Willa Mae," they said.

"See you in Sunday school," Marilee called over her shoulder.

"Let's find Rose and go," Nana said. "Your grandpa will be wondering where his dinner's at."

I took Nana's hand as we followed the sandstone fence. Aunty Rose said it was babyish the way I hung on to Nana. But I think she was just jealous.

We walked right by the mystery grave, close enough I could have reached out and touched the little white marker shaped like one of Moses' clay tablets.

I'd discovered the mystery grave one night when I was helping Grandpa and Nana mow the cemetery. I was chasing lightning bugs and nearly fell right over it.

BABY CLARK
BORN AND DIED NOVEMBER 23, 1941

That was almost the same time my mama died. But I didn't remember a baby. And if it was Mama's baby, why would it be stuck way over by the fence all by itself without

17

even a name? *The mystery baby* was how I'd come to think of her.

Him?

A name would have helped with that part.

"Nana, was Baby Clark a her or a him?"

The words came out of my mouth without me giving them permission. They just marched right out, naked in the sunshine.

I looked across the cemetery to Mama's angel, wondering if I'd be turned to stone for asking.

Nana stopped with a jolt, like she'd bumped into an invisible wall. Finally she said, "Baby Clark died," and then she went on walking, leading me by the hand as if we were in a big hurry.

"Yes, ma'am," I said. "That's why he or she has been buried in the cemetery."

Nana shut her eyes, and I felt bad for being smart. But probably everybody knew except me.

Sometimes I hated being wrapped up in a cotton candy cocoon, with people standing around waiting for me to turn into a beautiful butterfly like my mama.

Chapter 2

On the way home, Nana stared out the window, not saying a word. Aunty Rose had to crawl along in low gear because the REA machinery had cut up the road so bad.

I'd heard Grandpa say the Rural Electrification Association board in southern Illinois had pledged to have highlines along all the roads by this time next year. I couldn't wait. It would mean I wouldn't have to help Nana clean the oil lamps every morning if we got the electricity that everybody was talking so big about.

When we stopped the car under the hickory tree, Nana looked toward the machine shed, where we could hear Grandpa pinging and pounding.

It was about time for our midday meal, so I wasn't surprised when she said, "Help Rose start dinner." She touched my shoulder. "I'll be in directly"—which was Nana's way of telling me not to tag along when she went to talk to Grandpa.

Had she seen Grandmother Clark reading the letter to me? Had my question about the mystery baby upset her? Or was it just going to Mama's grave and putting all those pretty flowers around it?

In the kitchen, which always smelled of wood smoke from the cookstove, I hopped up to sit on the counter. I swung my legs like Aunty Rose had done when she was sitting on the fence by Joe.

"What do you think you're doing?" Aunty Rose said. "Mom said for you to help."

"I'm practicing flirting," I said, holding my feet out and staring at them through half closed eyes.

Aunty Rose giggled. "You're not doing it right. Sometime I'll show you. But come on now. Dad'll be wanting his dinner. You set the table while I start the potatoes."

She got six potatoes out of the tow sack under the washstand curtain, then dipped a pan of water from the bucket at the end of the counter.

"I'll set the table in a little bit. But before Nana comes back, I've got a question."

"Shoot," she said.

I think Aunty Rose expected my question to be about private girl stuff because her eyes widened when I asked, "Do you remember my daddy?"

It took her a minute to get used to the question, but then she answered, "Well, of course I do." Still holding the paring knife, she pushed away a lock of wavy hair with the back of her hand. "I was ten when . . ."

She peeled a circle around the potato, and I hitched up my socks while we waited for the never spoken words *your mama died* to march past.

". . . so I remember your daddy pretty good."

She picked up the second potato. "What brings that up?" she asked.

"Well, when we were at the cemetery, Grandmother Clark mentioned he might be getting tired of the navy."

"Well, that could be," Aunty Rose responded. "Eight years is a long time."

I twisted around to look out the window, watching for Nana.

"Where do you think he'd live?" I asked. "If he wasn't in the navy."

21

Aunty Rose shrugged. "Anywhere in the whole wide world, I guess. I suppose Harold has seen a lot of it by now."

"Did he ever live here?" I asked.

I thought I remembered something like that. All of us together in this house—Grandpa, Nana, Aunty Rose, Mama, and my daddy and me. But I might have dreamed it.

"Of course," Aunty Rose said. "Harold and your mama went through school together. His family has always lived on the old toll road."

Did Aunty Rose not understand my question? Or did she just not want to tell me?

I fidgeted with the curtain tieback, keeping an eye out for Nana, who didn't need to know how curious I was.

"Well, did you like him?" I asked, then counted the ten robins pecking among the bean rows as if the answer didn't matter much.

"Well . . . yes. I liked him all right." She glanced out the window too. "I liked Harold just fine."

"What was he like?" I said.

"Don't you remember anything at all?"

"Shhh," I warned, seeing Nana coming around the corner of the smokehouse.

All I remembered about my daddy was how much I

liked hearing him sing. But I wouldn't have known him by sight if I'd met him on the street in front of Montgomery Ward.

Aunty Rose started peeling the potatoes faster.

"Hurry," I whispered. "In five words or less. What's he like?"

Aunty Rose shrugged. "Nice," she whispered. Then she added, "But different from us."

I slid off the counter and got four dinner plates from the sideboard and started setting them around the dining-room table.

The screen door banged as Nana came into the kitchen.

I gazed at my face in the smooth china before I put the last plate down at Grandpa's place. I recognized Mama's eyes in the reflection. Were any of my features like my daddy's?

When Grandpa came in, carrying a full bucket of water from the well, he was whistling. He held my hands between his over the granite washbasin, and we rolled the Lifebuoy soap over and around, tangling our fingers. The smell of tractor oil wafted off his overalls.

Aunty Rose said I was too old to be washing up with Grandpa. But I didn't care.

Grandpa settled in the dining room to listen to the

noonday news as Aunty Rose and I passed back and forth from the kitchen, setting things on the table. The rich, greasy peppered smell of frying potatoes filled the air.

Grandpa stared at the curlicues in the blue wallpaper, not seeing a thing, his mind set on the announcer's words coming out of the radio on the sideboard.

We knew to be quiet so Grandpa could listen.

When the war was still on, we'd all hunkered around the radio for the noonday news because that was when they said the names of any of the boys from around Huxley, Illinois, who'd been killed in action. Sometimes we'd hear the names of those who were home on leave for a few days before going back to the front. And as the war ended, we'd listened to the names of those who'd finally come home for good.

I used to wonder a little about my daddy—wonder if I'd hear his name on the noonday news. But I never did.

"Somebody better go down to the cellar and get a jar of lima beans," Nana said. She was spreading leftover bacon from breakfast in a skillet to warm.

For once, without complaining that her name wasn't *Somebody,* Aunty Rose lit the oil lamp that we kept on the wood box by the cellar door.

"I'll go with you," I said, knowing that Aunty Rose still got the willies going down in the cellar by herself.

"Leave the door open behind us," Aunty Rose said. Then she started down the steps, which were just warped planks nailed crossways. She held the lamp high, and I clutched her blouse sleeve, following close behind.

"Don't," she said, shrugging my hand away. "You might make me fall."

We'd heard a thousand times about Nan Yarborough, who fell down the cellar steps and broke her neck.

"Well, don't go so fast," I said as the planks wobbled under my feet.

The damp concrete walls, the dirt floor, and vegetables aging in their bins gave off the cool smell of decay.

When we reached the bottom of the stairs, my foot came down on something that spurted out a vile smell.

"Oh, yuck!" I said, high stepping into the darkness. "I stepped on something!"

"Show me." Aunty Rose bent down with the lamp. "It was probably just a stinkbug."

"It was at least ten thousand times bigger than any old stinkbug," I said.

"Oh, it's only a rotten potato." She kicked it under the steps and flashed the light ahead. "Come on."

The shelves that Grandpa had built for Nana's canned goods loomed in the shadows of the southeast corner.

Quarts and pints of canned corn, green beans, yellow beans, lima beans, navy beans, tomatoes, peaches, blackberries, gooseberries, apples, applesauce, apple butter, cherries, chicken, mincemeat, and pear honey stood in dusty rows, two deep.

"You can get the beans," I told Aunty Rose, thinking of the silver-dollar-sized spiders that hopped around in the darkness.

She held the lamp low to pick out the yellow-green shine of the lima bean jars.

"You're such a baby," she said.

From the bottom of the stairs, the kitchen doorway at the top glowed. We went up the stairs faster than we'd come down. Aunty Rose even let me hang on to her skirt.

"What took you so long?" Nana said, looking up from turning the frying potatoes. "Are we getting low on lima beans?"

"No, Mom. There's plenty. We were just looking around."

Nana leveled her gaze on us, but she didn't say anything. I went out on the back steps to clean the potato mess from my shoe with a twig.

In a few minutes, Grandpa switched off the radio in the dining room, signaling that we should take up the food.

After we sat down at the table, we bowed our heads while Grandpa talked to God. Every day he said the same thing, the mysterious *semma, semma, summa table*, ending with *amen*.

Whatever Grandpa and God said to each other, it sure made the food taste good.

"Did you get the harrow fixed, Dad?" Aunty Rose asked.

"No. I'll get one of Retus's boys to come over and help me. They're good hands at fixing machinery. I'm going to plow the bottom ground down by the creek this afternoon."

Nana frowned. "Are you fixing to plant in the bottom? The corn got washed out last year."

Grandpa didn't say anything. Then, after a bit, he asked who we'd seen down at the cemetery. Nana told him about Wren Roberts and the Keifers and Mrs. Miller and her brood.

I watched Nana's and Grandpa's faces, wondering if Nana had told Grandpa I'd been talking to Grandmother Clark. Aunty Rose caught my eye, and I knew she was reading my mind. I would rather have cut off my tongue and hung it on the clothesline than let Grandpa know I had been asking questions about my daddy.

"Can I go with you, Grandpa?" I asked. "Down to plow the bottom?" The low ground lay along the edges of the creek where I liked to wade.

"That depends on what your grandma says," he answered, running a crust of biscuit left over from breakfast around his plate to sop up the last of the bean juice. But I could tell by the surge of light in his blue eyes that he was glad I'd asked.

"I don't want the girls going out to the field," Nana said. "Not around machinery. They could get hurt."

"But I like the creek," I protested.

I loved wading on the sandy, pebbly bottom, feeling the cool water swirl around my calves.

"Maybe I'll take you down Sunday afternoon," Grandpa said.

After dinner was over, Aunty Rose and I washed dishes in the pan of water Nana had left heating on the stove. We heard the blasting of the tractor starting in the machine shed, then the sound disappeared over the hills as Grandpa pulled the plow down to the creek.

Later, I felt butterflies in my stomach trying to get out for some reason, and Nana fixed me baking soda in water. Then she got a sick headache herself and had to lie on the davenport in the dim front room with a wet washrag over her eyes. And Aunty Rose nearly drove us nuts playing the windup phonograph and jitterbugging all over the house.

I lay on my bed and paged through the Sears Roebuck catalog, memorizing the pages of girls' clothing and marking the dresses I'd ask Nana to copy. I picked out some blue-and-white-checked material that maybe she would order and make up into a new Sunday dress, which I was needing, since it seemed like I'd shot three inches straight up since Christmas.

I mused through the pages with electric lamps and electric irons, wondering if we'd ever need such things.

Later on, I helped Aunty Rose wash her hair, pouring water from the gray-speckled granite pitcher through her waves as she hung her head over the washbasin. Then she washed my hair, circling her fingers on my scalp until I thought my knees would melt, it felt so good.

We sat on a quilt under the hickory tree and combed out our tangles. Jacky lay beside us in the grass, and I petted him with my toes.

"You're a good dog," I told him.

As Aunty Rose's long, thick brown hair dried, natural waves began to rise and fall in it.

"I wish I had hair like yours," I said.

"You've got hair like your mama's."

What I had was baby-fine light-colored hair that bleached out pale as silk in the summer.

Every now and then we'd hear the tractor rumbling down in the bottom. Once we heard a car pass, then toot as it went over the hill.

"I bet some of Dad's sheep are in the road," Aunty Rose said.

There was no use in trying to get the sheep back in the pasture. They'd follow Grandpa like ducklings behind a mother duck, but they'd just run from the rest of us.

The sound of the treadle sewing machine stopping and starting came through the open sunroom windows. I inched closer to Aunty Rose so I could talk quietly. Jacky whined and flopped his tail when I moved out of petting range.

"Do I look mainly like my mama or my daddy?" I asked, holding my breath.

"You don't look a bit like your daddy," Aunty Rose said, shutting her eyes as she tugged the comb through a tangle deep in her hair. "Not that I can see, anyway. Do you reckon Charles Michael will take me to Walnut Hill to the dance tomorrow night?"

30

"Why does everybody act like my daddy doesn't exist?" I asked.

Aunty Rose bent forward, hanging her head between her knees and brushing her hair over the top of her head. I knew she was hiding under there.

Jacky inched onto the quilt, back into the range of my toes, and I ran them through the thick fur on his side, leaving tracks.

Aunty Rose sat up, flipping back her hair. Her face was red—whether from hanging her head down or from my questions, I couldn't tell.

"Your daddy isn't a bad man," she said. "He just doesn't have anything to do with us. So why do you keep asking? All that was a long time ago." She stood up, running the brush through her hair again. "I'm going in to cut out that new blouse."

Aunty Rose walked away, a damp towel draped over her shoulder. I rolled over on my back and looked up at the little triangles of blue sky dancing through the leaves of the hickory tree. Someday I'd be a grown-up, and I'd make them tell me things.

"Fetch, Jack," I said, sitting up and throwing a broken twig across the yard. But he just rolled over on his back too and squirmed in the grass.

About dark, Grandpa came in from the field, and Nana had supper all ready. She'd baked a blackberry cobbler that still bubbled a little with steam, and we spooned Old Jerse's thick, clotted cream over it. In the soft lamplight, I listened to two whippoorwills talking to each other across the garden and let go of what was worrying me. Aunty Rose was right. Who cared about that old stuff?

Chapter 3

We didn't get to the creek that Sunday because a light rain started to fall right after church and kept on all day. And the following Sunday the preacher and his wife—Mr. and Mrs. Bradley—came to dinner, which required a mountain of work.

On Saturday, Aunty Rose and I cleaned like hired girls. We polished furniture until the house reeked of lemon oil. We scrubbed windows with vinegar water until they sparkled. And Aunty Rose ironed the white damask tablecloth until the Blessed Savior himself could have taken a meal off it.

Grandpa teased Nana that maybe he should build a new outhouse special for the preacher and his wife.

While Aunty Rose and I were slaving away, Nana made an angel food cake and two mincemeat pies to cap off her meal of fresh fried chicken, peas and new potatoes from the garden, noodle kugel, biscuits, canned applesauce, and enough lemonade to float a battleship.

And then, of course, after dinner on Sunday, the Bradleys stayed, talking on and on in the front room. I thought they might enjoy going down to the creek, but Nana said they wouldn't.

About three o'clock they went to rest on Nana and Grandpa's bed until it was time to get up for a light supper and go back to the church for the evening preaching. We didn't usually go to evening preaching. In the summer, if the skies were clear, we lay in the grass and studied the stars. Grandpa said we could see God in the Big Dipper better than we could see him at the church house.

But when the preacher came to Sunday dinner, we went to evening preaching.

From my point of view, the only thing good about the Bradleys' coming was that they wouldn't be back until February. We had just over thirty families in the Panther Fork congregation to feed the preacher on Sundays, so we could keep him nourished for about eight months without any repeats.

❧   ❧   ❧

The third weekend in June, my hopes rose for finally getting to Panther Fork Creek. On Saturday, it didn't look the least bit like rain. I studied the sky as we drove along County Line Road on the way to Lorrimer's store to do our Saturday trading.

"Remember about going to the creek tomorrow, Grandpa?" I said, pulling myself up to rest my chin on his shoulder.

"I remember," he said, shifting into low to get through the ruts.

"Looks like they could be kinder to the roads," Nana said. "We can't hardly get through, the way those trucks and Caterpillars cut things up."

"But think of the electricity, Mom," Aunty Rose said. "When we get it, we'll be able to just switch on the light."

Grandpa's blue eyes watched Aunty Rose in the rearview mirror. Grandpa wasn't sold on electricity.

"Think of having a refrigerator, Grandpa," I said. "We could have ice cubes, and ice cream, and ice-cold lemonade."

I'd had those things in Huxley when we went to visit our cousins. When we took the ice cubes out of the tray,

35

they cracked and sparkled like cut diamonds. And we ate striped ice cream that came from the store in a box. We sliced the ice cream like bread and laid it out on chilled plates with mint leaves from Aunt Patty's window box.

"We'll see," Grandpa said.

That was all he ever said about the electricity. *We'll see.*

There were four other cars at Lorrimer's and some men standing on the porch. Grandpa got Nana's crate of eggs out of the trunk and carried it in for her.

Lorrimer's smelled like chicken feed and Sugar Babies and the sizing that made the material Mrs. Lorrimer kept in the front so stiff and shiny.

"Look," I said to Aunty Rose as the screen door banged behind us. "They've still got that pink stripe."

"I don't want it anymore," Aunty Rose said, brushing the candy-striped fabric with her fingers and turning up her nose. "Charles Michael says he wants me to wear red."

"Some old bull might get after you," I said. "Better stay out of Charley Hoyt's pasture."

Everybody knew Hoyt had the meanest bull in southern Illinois, so I was giving good advice. But Aunty Rose just cut me a look and went on over to talk to Mary Carmichael, who rode the bus with her to Huxley High School.

Nana came back to where I was, putting her egg money in an envelope, which she tucked into the depths of her pocketbook. Nana was saving her egg money to buy new wallpaper for the front room.

"How much you got to go?" I asked.

"About five dollars is all," she said, trying to smooth down my hair.

I went out to where Mr. Carmichael was helping Grandpa load chicken mash into the trunk of our car. Grandpa was taller than the other men. He was slender, with a smooth face and deep blue eyes, and handsome enough to be a movie star.

He slammed down the trunk lid, making the dust fly, and gave me three nickels from his overalls pocket.

"Thank you," I said.

I gave one of the nickels to Nana and one to Aunty Rose. Then I handed over my own to Mrs. Lorrimer, who told me to help myself.

I buried my hand in the icy water of the cooler, making the pop bottles rattle as I searched for a strawberry pop. When I got it, I went out to sit on the porch in one of the metal chairs.

A man I didn't know was standing with his foot up on the running board of a car, talking to Bert Tiller.

"—said he was coming back. Didn't say when exactly. But I guess he's aiming to stay, because he was asking about jobs."

"Shoot," Bert said. "I've not seen Harold Clark in so long, I might not know him on the street."

The strawberry pop went up my nose, and I coughed like I was drowning.

The men looked up at me, and Bert's face turned red. I think he'd forgotten Harold Clark was my daddy until that very minute.

"How you doing, Willa Mae?" he asked.

"Fine," I whispered through my choking. "How are you?"

"I'm good," he said. "Howdy, Will." And his face turned even redder as he came up the steps and disappeared through the door without meeting Grandpa's eyes.

Grandpa sat down in the chair by me. Suddenly it was so still, I heard a rooster carrying on about a mile off.

Finally he said, "Pop's good," and took a swig.

"It sure is," I said. But I was afraid to drink any more lest I choke again.

Grandpa sat right there by me until Nana and Aunty Rose got through with their business. The Neills and the

Reileys pulled in while we were waiting and passed the time of day before they went in the store. The grown-ups seemed to look at me with more interest than usual, but if they had anything to say about my daddy, they were afraid to say it in front of Grandpa.

Grandpa went inside to settle up the bill, and I went right along with him, acting just as natural and happy as you please.

Not a word was mentioned on the ride home, but Nana went so far out of her way to act chipper that she made the butterflies start up in my stomach.

Grandpa spent the afternoon sorting out the sheep and moving them from one pasture to the next. Then I heard him pounding as he mended fence. Nana bent over the beans in the garden, moving slowly down the rows.

I helped Aunty Rose pin a dress pattern to some solid red material that Nana had let her get at Lorrimer's. Aunty Rose acted like her usual self, so I guessed she hadn't heard the talk, and I didn't bring it up.

That night, after supper and after Aunty Rose and Charles Michael had left for Huxley to see a movie, Nana spread a towel on my dressing table and carried in two pans of warm water for my bath. And though it wasn't quite dark yet, she brought in a lamp.

"So you can see all the dirt," she said, tracing my cheek with her finger.

After she left, I stripped off my clothes and started washing at the top and worked my way down to the bottom. I used one pan for the soapy washcloth and the other pan for the final rinsing. When I had finished except for my feet, I moved the soapy water to the floor and sat on the vanity bench soaking them, wiggling my toes in the warm water, wondering if Grandpa would still take me to the creek tomorrow.

As I lay in bed a little while later, smelling the fragrance of the Camay soap on my skin and the sunshine in the clean nightgown I'd put on, I eavesdropped through the bedroom wall just like always.

The springs squeaked as Nana sat on the edge of the bed to take off her shoes.

". . . Sure had a lot to say about Harold." Nana's voice grew strong as she moved to the wardrobe. Her shoes made a clunking sound as she dropped them inside.

"Harold Clark ain't worth shooting." Grandpa's voice came low from his side of the bed against the wall.

My toes curled back and my legs tensed under the sheet at Grandpa's harsh words.

"Be that as it may. . . ." Then I couldn't hear what Nana said as she turned toward the dresser on the opposite wall and started to brush her hair.

". . . One thing's sure. . . ." Her voice got louder again. "If he comes back, he'll want to take Willa Mae. . . ." And about that time a cricket started screeching right outside my window and I couldn't hear anything else.

Take me where?

I sure wished that old cricket would shut up. I knew he would eventually, and I decided to stay awake until he did so maybe I could hear the rest of the conversation and find out where Nana thought my daddy might take me.

But the next thing I knew sun was creeping across the bay window seat and the sheers swung out a little in the morning breeze.

We had to hurry through breakfast. Afterward, Grandpa, shaved and wearing his white shirt, studied his Sunday school lesson at the dining-room table. The rest of us rushed around getting the dishes done up, the lamp wicks trimmed, the globes washed, and the bedside pots emptied in the ash pile outdoors.

I didn't have much to do to get ready except pull one of my Sunday dresses over my head, put on clean anklets, and step into my new saddle oxfords. So when I was done, I sat down in a rocker in the front room, staring at Nana's closed bedroom door, wondering exactly what she was doing that took so long.

Eventually she would come out smelling of lilac dusting powder, her lips as red as a lady cardinal's. When I hugged her, her body would feel firm because of the foundation garments she wore under her black Sunday dress.

Overhead, Aunty Rose made the floor squeak as she moved around, passing from wardrobe to dressing table and back.

Finally we got in the Packard and headed down to Panther Fork Christian Church, where the preacher and his wife stood on the steps to shake our hands as we went in the front door.

I went forward to sit between Nana and Grandpa, just like always, in the second row. Aunty Rose stayed with the young people back by the door. She said I could start sitting there about any time, but if she thought I was going to be in the same pew as Petey Tyler, she was nuts.

After the opening song, followed by the prayer hymn, Grandpa talked to God while we all stood with our heads bowed. Of all the deacons and elders who took turns praying on Sunday morning, Grandpa did the best job of making a person feel like we had God's attention for the moment and He was truly listening to our needs and joys.

Everything went just fine until I got into Sunday school class. That's when Mrs. Mundey said to me, right in front of everybody, that she understood my daddy was coming home soon.

She said, "Willa Mae, I'll bet that sure warms your heart, don't it? To think of having your daddy home after all this time?"

"Yes, ma'am," I said, my cheeks stinging and my fingers crossed behind my back.

"How long has it been?" she asked.

I shook my head, not wanting to answer.

"Have you heard yet just exactly when he's coming?" she asked.

"Not just exactly," I said, thinking Mrs. Mundey was dumb as a sack of rocks not to see I didn't want to talk about it right there.

When we went around the room taking turns reading the Bible verses that were a part of our lesson, I'd lost my place and Marilee had to point me to John 3:16.

After Sunday school, during the preaching and the passing around of the bread and wine, I felt people's eyes on the back of my head as I sat in my place between Nana and Grandpa.

Leaving the church after services, I stuck close to Grandpa, knowing I was safe from the talk there.

Outside, God had lowered a piece of heaven down to cover Panther Fork. The sweet, soapy smell of roses from the front yard of the parsonage drifted by, and a breeze caught the skirt of my sailor dress as I went down the church house steps. Big sails of white clouds blew by. And across the road in the cemetery, Mama's angel looked over the hill, blessing us.

As we rode back, I wondered if what folks were saying about my daddy was true. I wondered, but I didn't talk about it.

At home, I changed into an everyday dress and went to help fix our Sunday dinner.

"I'll drop the noodles in," I offered, standing beside Nana at the stove.

"You do that, and I'll mash the potatoes," Nana said, catching a line of sweat running down her cheek. "Rose, you go to the garden for radishes. Red and white both."

The flowered noodle curls fattened up, bubbling the broth, as I dropped them in.

The old hen that Grandpa had lopped the head off of last night and Nana had dressed was cooking in the big iron skillet.

"Better stir those noodles, or they'll stick," Nana said, catching me watching Grandpa in the sunroom, still in his Sunday pants and white shirt, reading his New Testament with the words of Jesus printed in red, still without one whisker twitch of acknowledgment about my daddy's coming.

In a few minutes, Nana handed me the bowl of mashed potatoes to set on the table.

Steam fogged my face, giving off a smell of fresh butter. I ran my finger along the edge of the bowl, finding the little chip that had always been there. Then I set it between the salt and pepper shakers shaped like robins that stayed on the table for every meal.

I stood in the screened doorway, feeling the breeze dry the sweat on my arms. Jacky saw me and flopped his tail, but he didn't stir from the shade of the hickory tree.

Out in the garden, Aunty Rose jitterbugged down a bean row and swooped up a handful of radishes at the end.

"Wash up," Nana told Grandpa. "It's about ready."

After dinner, as we were stacking the dishes, a car horn sounded in the drive and I ran and pulled back the curtain. But it was only Charles Michael and some other boys that followed Aunty Rose around.

"Mom, don't let her stare out the window," Aunty Rose said over her shoulder as she went out the door.

Just to spite her, I pulled the curtain back and had a good look.

Aunty Rose smoothed down her skirt and made her hair bounce in the sunshine.

"—Spring Lake?" I heard Charles Michael ask.

After Aunty Rose left, I drifted into my bedroom and flopped down on the bed, staring at the roses on my wallpaper.

Why had my daddy vanished six years ago? Why hadn't he come home when Mama died? Why hadn't he written? Why did Grandpa hate him?

Then I started again at the beginning of my question list, picking at the chenille flowers on my bedspread. I heard Grandpa through the wall, squeaking out the little rod where he hung his tie, getting ready to go to the creek.

I went to find Nana, who was on the back porch putting on old shoes.

"You going to wear a hat?" she asked.

I shook my head.

"You'll get freckles."

Grandpa came out and stepped into his boots.

"We'll ride on the tractor," he said as he laced them up. "There's weeds too high to walk through in the back pasture."

Nana, in her sun hat, sat on one fender of the tractor. I climbed on the other fender, my feet up on Grandpa's toolbox.

"Hang on," Nana instructed me. Then she told Grandpa, "Go slow."

The tangy smell of tractor oil tickled my nose as Grandpa drove slowly through the pasture, going around the cow patties when he could. We went gradually up, cresting one hill and then another, and finally began the long crawl down.

Where Grandpa hadn't pastured the cattle, I could reach out and snap off the seed heads of the grasses, but Nana shook her head and motioned for me to hold on to the edge of the fender.

At the bottom of the last hill, Panther Fork made a shiny gray ribbon through the trees that lined its bank. We stayed to the tall grass, skirting the plot Grandpa had planted with corn, in spite of Nana's advice.

Grandpa stopped the tractor in the shade. Two trees had spread their branches so wild grapevine crossed from one tree to the other, making a natural arched doorway to the creek.

We went single file, Grandpa in the lead, mashing down the grass for Nana and me. The scribble of a blue racer snake flickered through the grass.

The rising and falling creek had cut sandy steps in the bank. I ran down them, pulling off my shoes and socks. The cold water gurgled as it broke its path to go around my legs, and the coarse sand on the bottom clasped my feet as if it had missed me.

"Feels good, don't it?" Nana asked, standing calf deep in the water, holding her skirt bunched in front of her.

My skirt was already soaked around the bottom, the line of wetness inching higher and higher.

Grandpa was rolling up the legs of his overalls as high as they would go, which was a promise of serious wading.

"Can we go up to the rock dome?" I asked.

Grandpa looked at the creek, assessing its depth. "Should be about right," he said. "We may get a little wet."

"I'll wait," Nana said. "You two are going to come back soaked to your armpits."

That was exactly what I hoped for, but I kept still.

"Won't be gone long," Grandpa told Nana, leading the way upstream.

Nana was right. Three bends in the creek later, the waterline on my dress came up to the armholes, and Grandpa was wet to the waist. But that was because of the drop-off right before the dome, which we both knew was there but pretended to have forgotten.

The sandstone dome, mapped with crack lines and blue-green mineral deposits, arched over our heads like an upside-down bowl. People had written or scratched their names, some up so high, I wondered how they got there. *Joseph Mueller, January 4, 1849. Dodie Hender, 1907. Mellie Brown, August 7, 1922.*

We read the names out loud every time we came to the dome, and Grandpa always told me that Dodie Hender was young Doc Hender, who nursed people through the flu epidemic of 1918. He dropped dead of exhaustion in his buggy, but his horses went on home and carried him right up to the back door.

After he finished telling the story, he said, "Your Nana will start worrying. We better go back."

In a quiet patch downstream, Grandpa spotted a big old olive-colored snake, about four feet long, lazing in the shallows. We gave him a wide berth until we could get out of the creek. Once we were on the sandy bank, Grandpa pulled a forked branch off a tree, then started trimming the ends of the fork with his pocketknife.

"What are you doing?" I asked, watching him shape the branch into a thick, long-handled prong.

"Have you ever seen the inside of a water moccasin's mouth?" he asked.

My heart nearly jumped right out of my chest. Everybody knew moccasins were deadly poison. I shook my head.

"Well, we'll look," he told me. "It won't hurt the snake none."

And in a flash, before I could say, *Don't mess with that nasty old snake,* he slipped the fork over the head of the moccasin, sinking the prongs into the sand and pinning the snake, who thrashed like crazy for a minute, then lay still.

Careful as he could be, and my heart beating so hard I was practically bouncing up and down on the bank, Grandpa bent down and gripped the snake's head with his hand right behind the fork and lifted up the dangling length of it.

The snake opened its mouth, and Grandpa held its head so firm, I saw the tendons in his forearm stand out. I'd never seen such a wide-open, dangerous-looking, white, cottony depth in all my life, and I knew for certain why they were called cottonmouth water moccasins.

"Ain't that something?" Grandpa said.

I nodded.

He put the snake back in the water, pinned its head hard with the forked stick, stepped up on the bank, and let it go. The snake shot off downstream.

"You don't see many cottonmouths around here," Grandpa said. "Only seen seven or eight in my whole life. But they're something to look out for."

The water didn't feel so comfortable to me as we finished our trip, and I kept watching the swirls and shadows.

"You don't need to be afraid," Grandpa said, reading my mind. "You just need to be careful."

As Nana came into view around the bend, he said, "We won't worry your Nana by telling her."

Nana was sitting on the bank, her bottom buried in sand and her feet dangling in the water. The water moccasin had probably swum right by her.

I wouldn't tell, but I wished I could. I'd like everybody to know that my grandpa was the bravest man alive.

Chapter 4

The rest of June went by, and my daddy didn't turn up. Seemed like folks got tired of talking about it after a while, and even Nana and Grandpa stopped acting anxious. Or at least I didn't hear any more worrisome conversations through the bedroom wall.

Thinking about my twelfth birthday coming up took the place of thinking about my daddy.

As the first week in July passed, the days turned hot and dusty. Panther Creek started to dry up, and Grandpa said he was able to walk parts of it. He told Nana he'd been smart, planting some of his corn in the cool, damp bottom ground.

He did temporary work for the REA, using his team to

help clear brush for the highline. They were working right down on Karse Road, which meant Grandpa could come home for dinner each day rather than carrying his lunch. He told us about the linemen who climbed up the tall poles like monkeys to install things called insulators that the electrical wire would hang on.

Aunty Rose and Nana and I hoped being exposed to so much electrical work would make Grandpa change his mind about wanting electricity.

"When the highline comes to our road, Dad, are you going to sign up for it?" Aunty Rose finally asked one day at the dinner table after Grandpa had contented himself on fresh, warm cherry pie.

We held our breath while he thought about it. I think Nana was contemplating the wonders of an electric stove, which she'd heard about the last time she went to Huxley. Aunty Rose wanted an electric iron so we wouldn't have to heat up our old flatirons on the woodstove on a hot day and change them five or six times to do up one of Grandpa's starched white shirts. I wanted a refrigerator so we could keep ice cream.

But Grandpa said, "I don't see why we can't get along with what we've got. We don't want for anything we really need."

Grandpa was right about that, but Nana said we could "have things a lot nicer" if we got the electricity.

Finally the thirteenth came, and Aunty Rose woke me up Sunday morning sitting on my bed and singing "Happy Birthday." Nana gave me a hug and a pinch of love to grow on when I went in the kitchen. And when Grandpa came in from milking, he got a 1935 silver dollar he'd been saving for me out of his bureau drawer.

At church, Uncle Retus's family was talking big about how they'd be getting a transformer put up at the end of their driveway, and Petey Tyler said his mama had already ordered a fluorescent floor lamp from the Jewel Tea man for $12.95.

I might have felt left out of the excitement, but when the Sunday school superintendent asked if there had been any birthdays this week, I got to go up and drop twelve pennies in the Birthday Bank.

When we got home, the black-eyed peas Nana had left simmering smelled so good, I asked everybody to please hurry so we could eat. Also, I knew a surprise angel food cake, ringed with maraschino cherries, was hiding on the top shelf of the cupboard, where Nana thought I wouldn't look.

The cake didn't turn up at dinner, so I figured Nana

was saving it for later. Grandpa had said he'd make ice cream in honor of my birthday, and he went outside and cranked the ice-cream maker while I helped Nana and Aunty Rose do the dishes.

By the time I got outside, Grandpa had covered the ice-cream maker with a burlap bag and left it in the shade so the ice cream would harden.

"How would you like to walk over and see the sheep?" he asked me.

I could see some of the sheep from where I stood. Several ewes with their spring lambs grazed on the hill.

But maybe Grandpa meant how would I like to see them up close. Sometimes, if he was nearby, the woolly lambs would let me touch the kinky topknots on their heads.

"I'd like that," I said.

As we walked toward the pasture, the dried-up grass crunched under our feet because of the lack of rain.

"You hear that, Grandpa?" I said, turning back to look at the northwest horizon. Maybe—just maybe—it was a shade darker than the rest of the sky, and maybe I had heard a rumble of thunder.

He nodded.

"Think it'll rain?"

"You never can tell," he said. But I saw hope in his eyes.

Grandpa opened the gate to the pasture, taking a bucket of mash for the lambs off a nail pounded high into the gatepost.

"I've been thinking to give you a lamb of your own to raise," he said.

I glanced at him in surprise, then looked away, acting like I was paying close attention to going through the gate, because it didn't seem decent letting another person see how proud that made me. Nana had her chickens. Aunty Rose had two hogs. And now I would have a sheep. Well, a lamb, really. But the lamb would grow into a sheep. And there was nothing finer than owning livestock.

The lambs rambled across the pasture, their hooves noisy on the dry, cracked ground. They saw the bucket of mash and scrambled to get their faces in it, bumping our legs and stepping on our feet while their mamas stood back, bleating nervously.

While one lamb had her nose in the bucket, I touched the thick wool on the top of her head, but she jumped back.

Eventually the lambs got their fill and ran to join their mamas.

"Did you see one you'd like to have?" Grandpa said,

dumping what little was left of the mash on the ground, which brought a few lambs trotting up again.

"I don't know good stock," I said, trying to sound responsible. "How can I tell? But I kind of like that one there with the black face." I pointed to the lamb that had come back to nuzzle the ground for the last traces of the mash.

Grandpa nodded. "She comes from a good mother." He tried to point the mama out, but in the mass of sheep I couldn't tell for sure which one she was.

"Good mothers usually have good lambs," he said. And the light in his eyes told me he was proud of the way I'd chosen.

Thunder rumbled louder in the northwest, and Grandpa and I smiled at each other.

I watched the darkening sky as we walked back toward the house. It was going to rain, the ice cream was ready to eat, I had a birthday cake waiting in the wings, and now I owned livestock.

I ran ahead to tell Nana and Aunty Rose what Grandpa had given me for my birthday. They acted all surprised, but they probably had their fingers crossed behind their backs.

We gathered up bowls and spoons, and Grandpa had the ice cream ready to dip by the time we got outside.

The storm front pushed a cool breeze ahead of it. Since the sun had slipped behind the clouds, we sat on the concrete platform around the well to eat. I tried to slow down and savor the moment, but the icy sweetness drove me on, my spoon pinging against the thick, cool crockery bowl in my hands.

"If you eat too fast, you'll get a headache," Nana said, touching my knee as we sat beside each other on the well curb.

In the pause between bites, I looked down the drive. A man in a white sailor suit waited there, watching us.

For a second, I thought lightning had hit nearby because he stood out in an eerie light. My foot went all cold where I dropped my ice-cream bowl as I stood.

I tried to tell Nana and Grandpa to look, but my voice box wouldn't work.

When Jacky came tearing around the machine shed, barking and growling, aiming down the drive like a bullet, Grandpa whirled around.

"Jack," Aunty Rose commanded, jumping up and slapping her thigh.

Jacky, whining, trotted back to sit by Grandpa's side. He gazed up at Grandpa's face, waiting for a signal.

I wanted a signal from Grandpa too, but he was no

more aware of my presence than of the little black ant crawling on his shirt collar. Grandpa had his feet planted apart and his arms at his side, his only movement a deep breath that made him look even bigger.

Nana, her lips still parted for a bite of ice cream, stared at the sailor.

Aunty Rose was so still, she could have been a picture of herself.

Nobody paid any attention to me.

"Daddy?"

I took one step toward him, then another.

"Daddy?"

But I couldn't have heard if he'd answered me because my heart was drumming so loud.

I got halfway down the drive, my legs trembling. Then I stopped and looked back at Aunty Rose, Nana, and Grandpa. Their faces brightened for an instant, then dimmed again as I turned back toward the sailor.

But wait.

He wasn't my daddy after all.

I stared at the man's coppery hair falling over a sweaty face and freckles spattered on every bit of his skin. He looked awful scrawny, with a big Adam's apple that bobbed up and down. And he was crying.

"Mae Bug?" he said, his voice hoarse.

Then he dropped his duffel to empty out his arms, and I ran into them, knowing he was my daddy after all.

"Mae Bug." He squeezed me, scratching my face with his whiskers. He smelled like dust and something else that I remembered from a long time ago.

He held me away from him. "What happened to my little girl? You got all tall and skinny on me. But look at that hair," he said, touching the top of my head.

Then I saw his bloodshot brown eyes settle on the people waiting for him under the hickory tree.

I looked, thinking Grandpa might turn away in contempt, but a gust of wind blew his hair back as he stood stiffly, like Jacky with the scent of an intruder.

Thunder rumbled more loudly.

Daddy's Adam's apple bobbed up and down, and his grip on my arm tightened probably more than he realized.

He brought his eyes back to mine.

"How are you?" he asked me, looking so deep that I felt tears starting to come.

I nodded. "Good," I whispered. "How are you?"

"Mighty glad to be home," he said. Then he pulled a handkerchief out and mopped the sweat off his forehead, wiping away tears at the same time.

He turned his back and blew his nose, and I didn't know what to do. I glanced at Grandpa. Could he tell Daddy was crying?

My family just stood there, holding their ice-cream bowls like they were glued to their hands. I wanted to be with them.

But I couldn't leave my daddy standing there by himself.

Finally he picked up his duffel and took my hand and we headed toward the shade.

When Daddy stuck his hand out to Grandpa, my heart nearly stopped.

Ignoring Daddy's gesture, Grandpa just nodded.

Daddy nodded back.

Then Daddy clasped Nana's hand, calling her Mae. And before he could shake hands with Aunty Rose, she gave him a hug that made him step back and smile. If I could have given Aunty Rose the whole world tied up in a pretty bow at that point, I'd have done it.

"We'll dip you some ice cream, Harold," Nana said. But that wasn't a serious sign of peace, because everyone knew you could count on Nana for hospitality.

"I could have been here sooner," Daddy said, addressing himself to everybody but Grandpa. "I got off the train in Huxley this morning and caught a ride to Hinner's Corner. Then I took a notion to come cross-country. So I've walked the last six miles."

His shoes were coated with dust, and his nose glowed with sunburn, but he was grinning at me.

I didn't know what else to do, so I pulled up my socks and grinned back.

"So what are you fixing to do now, Harold?" Grandpa said. He towered over my daddy, and his voice was colder than any ice cream I'd ever tasted.

Nana shot Grandpa a look.

"Well, I haven't seen my folks yet," Daddy said. "Need to get down there first thing. How about you, Mae Bug? Want to come along? Go visit your other grandparents?"

All on its own, my head bobbed up and down.

Daddy nodded toward the electric poles standing out on the horizon way over by Mick Pennington's place to the southwest.

"I see the rural electrification work has started up again now the war's over," he said, dipping into the ice cream that Nana handed him. "I just may wire some houses," he told Grandpa.

He licked the cream off his lips and smiled at me again.

"Ever wired a house?" Grandpa asked in a tone that said, *Ever walked on water?*

"Nope." Daddy rocked back on his heels. "But I learned electricity in the navy. That's what this badge means."

I looked at the globe he pointed to on his wrinkled white sleeve.

"Electrician." He spooned ice cream into his mouth. "I wired ships. I figure I can wire houses. At least they stay still."

He set his bowl down on the well curb, making the spoon clatter in the silence.

"Well, better take your nightgown, Mae Bug," he said, nodding at me. "Maybe we'll stay at my folks' for a few days. Then I'll see if I can find us a place to live."

Grandpa jerked as if somebody had stabbed him with the pitchfork. Nana made a choking sound, and Aunty Rose gripped my shoulder.

Thunder rolled over the pond dam, banging closer.

Would Grandpa shoot Daddy?

Nana smoothed her skirt with both hands and her voice shook. "She's slept right here every night that she can remember, Harold."

That was true. And I felt my toes curl down to grip the earth.

"Now, Mae, I'll take good care of her," Daddy told Nana. Then he turned to me. "We'd better shove off, Mae Bug."

"Storm's coming," I said. "We better get inside."

I pushed for the house, not knowing what else to do. I ran straight through to the sunroom and probably would have kept on going if the walls and windows hadn't stopped me.

I stood watching the light, which had gone all queer, since the blackness of the storm was coming in from the north, but the sun was still shining in the south.

The screen door banged, and Nana's patient, steady footsteps moved around the kitchen.

I listened.

What was Nana doing?

My hands left damp prints on the window frame when I took them away. As I watched the smudges evaporate, I hung on Nana's every footstep.

When I couldn't stand it any longer, I went to find her.

"Reckon I'll have to light a lamp if it gets much darker," Nana said, setting my surprise birthday cake in a box.

"Why are you doing that?" I cried.

"You can take it down to Harold's folks'," Nana said, reaching to cradle my face in her hands.

I smelled the sweetness of the ice cream and cake icing on her fingers. I tried to shake my head *no*.

"The cake will taste just as good there," she said. "You'll see."

No, it wouldn't. It was a birthday cake for here. Not there.

But she turned to put the lid on the box and started tying it up with string.

The curtains billowed over the washstand and lightning slashed the sky behind the pond dam.

"Why don't they come in?" I asked, watching Aunty Rose and my daddy out the window and worrying the lightning would get them. They stood by the old Packard. Wind whipped Aunty Rose's skirt between her legs and snapped my daddy's dark sailor tie over his shoulder.

"Rose is going to drive you and your daddy down to Harold's folks'," Nana said. "We got it all worked out. If you hurry, you can beat the storm."

Where was Grandpa?

Nana held the boxed cake out to me.

I shook my head. "I don't want to go."

She set the box back on the counter and drew me to her. "Maybe you do and maybe you don't," she said. "But it's best to go ahead with what you told your daddy."

She squeezed me, then left me standing by the awful cake box as she walked through the dining room to the sunroom. She came back with her sewing basket. "I meant to give you these at bedtime," she said, lifting the lid.

Nana held up a pair of pink cotton pajamas banded around the collar and cuffs with pink satin. They were identical to the pair Nana had made Aunty Rose for her birthday back in May.

If my daddy hadn't come home, tonight Aunty Rose and I would have put on our twin pajamas and polished each other's toenails. But now everything was different.

Nana folded the pajamas and laid them on top of the cake box.

"You'll have something new to sleep in tonight," she said.

I clenched my teeth. Why was Nana packing me off like this?

And where was Grandpa? I thought sure he would do something if my daddy tried to take me away. But he'd just slapped on his cap and headed for the sheep shed. I'd seen him crossing the road when I was looking out the sunroom windows.

"We better hurry," Nana said. "Don't want Rose to get caught in a gully washer."

She carried the cake box and pajamas in one arm and guided me with the other.

In no time Aunty Rose, my daddy, and I were getting in the car, me in the backseat by myself and Aunty Rose driving.

"Be good now," Nana said, shutting my door. "Don't be any bother."

Aunty Rose turned out of the drive, lightning crackling behind us and a gritty wind blasting us broadside.

Ignoring the storm, Grandpa strode through the pasture, the sheep parting before him like the Red Sea in front of Moses.

He didn't turn around to say good-bye until I leaned out the window and yelled, "I'll be back, Grandpa. Take care of my livestock."

He stopped then and wheeled around, waving.

The car swayed and bounced through the ruts from the Caterpillar tractors. But Aunty Rose still stayed ahead of the rain.

When we got to Grandmother and Grandfather Clark's, Aunt Belle came running to the car and threw her arms around my daddy before he could hardly get out the door. Grandfather Clark hung back, sucking his pipe, beaming. Grandmother Clark, tears trickling over her cheeks, squeezed Daddy's arms and stood studying him. Then she hugged him to her.

I got out and stood beside the car.

"And here's our Willa Mae come to visit," Grandmother Clark said, squeezing my shoulders with both hands.

Only when we were turning toward the house did she remember Aunty Rose. "Can you come in, Rose?" she asked. "Until the storm passes?"

"Mom's expecting me right back," Aunty Rose said. "But thanks anyway."

I held the cake box and my pink pajamas until the old Packard disappeared around the curve.

Chapter 5

As we walked toward the house, Grandmother Clark put her arm around my shoulders and kissed the top of my head. "How lucky we are you've come to visit us."

I caught my breath.

"Oh, Harold, we've not seen enough of her," Grandmother Clark sighed, wiping tears off her cheeks with her fingers. "She's half grown up and the spitting image of her mama. Some days I can't believe Treva's gone."

I gaped at Grandmother Clark. Didn't she know that nobody ever mentioned my mama's death outright like that?

"Me neither, Mom," Daddy said, the hoarseness of his

voice making me stare. His hand reached out as if he was trying to touch something that wasn't there, and the pale, drawn lines around his eyes pulled me over to stand by him. My arm brushed against his.

"Mama's happy in heaven," I said, swallowing, knowing Grandpa would be proud of the way I didn't cry. "We don't have to be sad."

I held the cake box out to Grandmother Clark. "Look. Nana sent angel food cake."

Grandmother Clark blinked. Then she smiled. "That was nice of Mae."

She took the cake from my hands. "Come on in," she said, turning to lead the way.

Grandfather Clark studied me, his lips curved around his pipe. Aunt Belle had an expression on her face like she'd found a fairy among the hollyhock roots. And my daddy was staring now as if I were a Cracker Jack toy and a fancy valentine all rolled into one. He put his hand on my head.

Butterflies started an uprising in my stomach. As I followed Grandmother Clark toward the house, I wished Aunty Rose had stayed a while to keep me company.

Tall trees, their limbs tossing in the wind of the oncoming storm, loomed over the house.

My feet remembered the sandstone path, exactly how far it was from one rock to the next and the wobbliness of the third rock from the porch.

Inside, the air was stifling from the cookstove, and so many things cooking threw their spices and sweetness into the air that my nose couldn't make sense of them.

"Been a long time since I've smelled food that good," my daddy said, taking a deep breath.

"Did they feed you in the navy, son?" Grandfather Clark asked.

"Not much." My daddy winked at me, then laid his hand on my head again.

"Well, your mother and sister would be sorry to hear that," Grandfather Clark said. "They've cooked enough to make up for several years of starvation."

"Oh, Dad, hush," Grandmother Clark said, opening the oven and lifting out a bubbling pie.

Daddy and I just stood in the middle of the kitchen, the others moving around us. Daddy's eyes flicked from one place to the next. He rocked on the balls of his feet, his hands inside his pockets.

"Is it just like you remember it, Harry?" Aunt Belle asked, drying a glass and setting it on the table.

"Well." My daddy shrugged, words not coming at first. "A person kind of forgets." Then, his eyes acknowledging he'd said the wrong thing, he told her, "But it's sure good to be home. Better than you know."

"Harold probably wants to wash up," Grandmother Clark said. "He looks dry and dusty."

"That's the truth," Daddy agreed. "I walked through Dinsmore Woods and came out north of the Shannons'. The country looks about the same. Except for the high-line wires."

Aunt Belle started setting plates on the square oilcloth-covered table. I remembered eating here, right in the kitchen, by the window that looked across the yard to a henhouse, watching the red chickens peck for bugs.

"I'll clean up on the back porch." My daddy walked through the room and out the door on the other side. "Still got that old straight razor, Dad?"

"Where it always was," Grandfather Clark said, following Daddy.

"I got out your civilian clothes, Harry," Aunt Belle called over her shoulder. "Starched them all up the way you like them."

My daddy tweaked a lock of her hair as he passed by.

She laughed and elbowed him away, but I could tell she was practically shaking with joy to see my daddy.

"It'll be a while till the meal is ready," Grandmother Clark told me, wiping her hands on her apron. "Why doesn't Belle cut you a piece of Mae's cake so you don't get hungry?"

My stomach felt about as hard as a walnut, but I nodded. At least eating would be something to do, though Nana would say I shouldn't spoil my appetite.

When Aunt Belle handed me the little plate, she said, "You're almost as tall as me now. The last time you came here, you were just a little thing."

"I'm twelve," I said. "Today."

She smiled, showing buckteeth. "I know. Happy birthday."

"Thank you."

I sat down at the table with the slice of cake, but I scooted the maraschino cherries aside because right now my stomach rolled at the idea of their syrupy sweetness.

The sounds of Daddy's splashing and Grandfather Clark's voice came from the back porch.

What was I supposed to do? At home, I would have

been helping Nana or Aunty Rose, but Grandmother Clark and Aunt Belle didn't seem to need my help.

A red hen squawked through the grass as Daddy tossed his wash pan of water into the yard.

"We've got kittens under the front porch," Grandmother Clark said.

"How many?" I asked.

"Four, last time I looked. The mama won't care if you take a peek."

I stood up, glad for an excuse to get out of the house.

"Just look behind the rain barrel," Grandmother Clark called.

Outside, the wind blew my hair back, and thunder rumbled steadily. Kneeling on the ground at the corner of the sloping porch, I made out the furry balls in the shadows. But the mama watched me with wary eyes, so I moved away.

On the south side of the house, my old rope swing still hung from a high tree branch. Half my life had passed since I'd twisted round and round in that swing.

Wisps of images snuck up on me—Mama sitting on the porch, stroking a gray cat, watching. I flipped up the seat of the swing. WMC was carved in the bottom just as I remembered.

I sat in it, twisting around, winding up the ropes. Then I leaned back and spun, my legs outstretched.

When the rain began to fall in hard drops, I darted for the house.

Inside, Grandmother Clark had already lit oil lamps, though the clock on the shelf said only four-thirty. Daddy was coming in the back door with his hair slicked and his face fresh and clean from shaving. In his gray shirt and trousers, he looked like the daddy I was starting to remember.

He picked up a chair and sat it down by me. "Cake pretty good?"

I took a bite. I was having cake with a stranger, and I was having cake with my daddy. I guess it tasted good.

"I remember Mae's cooking," my daddy said. "She still make biscuits and gravy for breakfast?"

"Every morning," I said. "Biscuits and gravy and bacon and eggs."

"Only sometimes she made steak back then." He polished off his piece of cake before I had taken three bites of mine. "After a butchering."

I gazed at the three uneaten cherries on my plate. If Daddy had been there for Nana's breakfasts, it must mean that there had been a time when Grandpa liked my daddy.

"Do you hate my grandpa?" I asked, meeting Daddy's eyes.

Maybe he would talk to me about important things and answer some of my questions.

His face bunched up, and he caught Grandmother Clark's eyes. She and Aunt Belle had frozen in place like they were playing statue. Only Grandfather Clark, who was in the back of the yard doing some chores around the henhouse, kept on with his business.

"Did Will tell you that?"

"No, sir," I said. Nobody told me anything. That was the problem. "I just wondered why I didn't hear from you for so long is all. I figured you must have hated somebody."

"I didn't hate anybody," my daddy protested.

Grandmother Clark and Aunt Belle started moving again.

"It's just. . . ." And my daddy broke off when Grandmother Clark passed behind his chair and squeezed his shoulder.

"It's just that we sure are glad to have you here, honey," Grandmother Clark said to me. "And everything will be all right now your daddy's home."

I didn't exactly see how my daddy's coming home made everything all right.

Grandfather Clark came in, and for an instant, his eyes widened at the sight of my daddy and me sitting at the table. Then he dropped his cap on the peg inside the door. "I opened up the flaps on the brooder house. It's a dry storm."

"We needed the rain," Grandmother Clark said.

The shower had wetted down the grass some, and a robin in the backyard worked at tugging a worm out of the ground. The air had a sweet smell. But the rumble of thunder was passing off to the southeast.

The table got more and more full as Grandmother Clark and Aunt Belle set steaming bowls and platters on it.

"I think we should have some wine, Mother," Grandfather Clark said. "To celebrate."

From a back bedroom, he brought a glass jug, twisting the top off as he came, and Grandmother Clark set out five glasses.

Five? Did they think I would drink wine? Grandpa said liquor was the devil's own trade. And Aunty Rose was fond of saying, *Lips that touch wine will never touch mine.*

"To Harold and Willa Mae," Grandfather Clark said, raising his glass.

Sitting on my hands, I stared at the glass of wine. Liquor was bad. Even the church wine used at the communion table was really just grape juice.

My daddy swallowed a mouthful, smacked his lips, and swallowed again.

"Good batch, Dad," he said.

I wondered if Daddy and the others would fall down drunk.

"I wish Les were here," Aunt Belle remarked.

"Les is my brother," Daddy told me. "You might not remember him. He went to Oklahoma before the war and stayed there." Then he noticed my untouched wineglass. "It's just Dad's dandelion wine, Mae Bug. It won't hurt you."

I felt my face flaming redder than the dots in Aunt Belle's apron, but Grandfather Clark smiled at me across the table and began to talk about the peach trees he'd set out.

Grandfather Clark's eyes were flecked with green just like my daddy's. I remembered once when I'd sat close to him and he'd read me a story about an eagle carrying a baby away to its aerie. The baby's mama had climbed the rocks and found her baby safe in the eagle's nest.

Over the years, I'd thought about the story, knowing how glad the mama must have been to have her child back in her arms.

"Do you remember the story about the eagle's nest?" I said.

He nodded. "I do. That's a good story."

We worked our way through the food, everything tasting better than I expected.

Finally, when pieces of cherry pie steamed in front of us and ruby-sweet juice oozed from the crust, Grandfather Clark lifted his hand and everybody sang me a birthday song.

At home, we didn't sing because we all sounded like sick cows, as Nana said. But the Clarks sounded almost as good as the radio.

I stared at my daddy, watching his face as the music bubbled up in him and overflowed onto me.

"Thank you," I said when they were done. "That was the prettiest song I ever heard."

They laughed as I blushed, but I didn't mind.

Everybody raved about Grandmother Clark's pie. When we were finished, I helped clear the table and wash dishes. By the time everything was put away, it was nine o'clock. Nobody had gotten drunk, but they'd laughed a lot, and now my daddy had tired lines carved in his face.

"I made up a cot for you in your daddy's room," Grandmother Clark said.

I told myself nobody died of sleeping in a strange bed as I followed Grandmother Clark to a bedroom not much bigger than Nana's cedar closet. A narrow bed occupied one corner and a sewing machine the other. A round table with claw feet, heaped with stacks of books, took up all the space in a third corner. A curtain that stopped several inches short of the floor covered the doorway we'd come through.

Grandmother Clark set the lamp on the sewing machine and turned back the covers on the cot. She smoothed the pillow. My new pajamas lay folded at the end of the cot.

"I hope you'll sleep all right," Grandmother Clark said.

I couldn't see her face very well. When I swallowed, my throat hurt.

"I will," I said, remembering Nana's instruction not to be any bother.

I had to sit on the cot and pull up my feet for Grandmother Clark to get past. She looked back at me, uncertainty clouding her face. Nana always gave me a hug and kiss before I went to sleep, but I hoped Grandmother Clark wouldn't.

"Good night," she said. "Call if you need anything. We'll all be turning in soon. I think your daddy is about ready to fall over."

I dimmed the lamp real low so nobody could see my

silhouette through the curtain as I pulled off my clothes and slipped on the pajamas. Then I crawled between the covers on the cot.

Beneath the pillow, something hard-edged touched my hand. Exploring with my fingers, I knew before I pulled it out that it was the book Grandfather Clark used to read to me.

I got out of bed and turned up the lamp.

Happy Birthday, Granddaughter was written inside the cover. *Now you can read your own stories.*

It was quiet in the kitchen, as if they were waiting. I felt dizzy with too many feelings, and my pajamas clung to my back.

Daddy and the Clarks were nice, but I wanted to go home.

I put out the lamp, slid the book safely under the cot, and lay back down.

In the other room, the grown-ups took up their conversation about rural electrification.

I pressed the corners of my eyes to stop the tears from staining Grandmother Clark's company pillowcase with the pretty embroidery. I lay still, not wanting to move on the cot, and my left foot fell asleep from where the cot frame pressed my ankle.

After a while, my daddy came back. I pretended to be sleeping as I listened to him taking off his clothes and hanging them on the pegs on the wall. Grandmother and Grandfather Clark and Aunt Belle made rustling sounds like birds bedding down for the night.

Finally it was so quiet, my ears ached, and I jumped when a fox yipped across the fields. My daddy groaned in his sleep and turned over. Wisps of memory stirred and I suddenly felt safe, but I missed Mama.

As I fell asleep, the cot seemed to sway and I floated into dreams. I couldn't remember them the next morning, but I woke up happy to see the sun's patterns on the wall. After breakfast, Daddy borrowed Grandfather Clark's old Model A Ford to take me home. I told the Clarks thank you for the book and said I'd enjoyed my visit. As I started to climb in the car, Grandmother Clark slipped her arm around me and planted a quick kiss on my head.

"Come back soon," she said. "When you can stay a while."

Things looked better in the sunshine, and I liked bouncing along the rutted roads beside Daddy. He didn't hardly slow down for the rough places and explained all the electrical stuff we passed.

"What I'd like to do, Mae Bug, is get a few jobs wiring houses right here. Folks around Panther Creek have known me since I was born. So it shouldn't be too hard finding work. Then soon as I get some money saved up, I can find us a place to live."

"But I've already got a place," I cut in, hoping it wouldn't hurt his feelings.

He nodded, but I couldn't tell if he was really listening.

Grandpa was in the field when we got home, and Nana was at the well, pumping a bucket of water. She stopped squeaking the pump handle and asked my daddy if he'd like a glass of tea.

But he said he needed to go talk to some people about finding work.

"I'll be back soon," he told me. "And we'll try to find some trouble to get into."

Nana made her mouth smile, but her eyes darkened. I could see her hand itching to reach out and draw me to her.

I felt like a little metal ball being pulled between two magnets.

"Bye," I said. "See you later." It was the best I could do with Nana standing right there.

As he turned toward the car he told Nana over his

shoulder, "I'd be glad to fix that pump, Mae. It's just a worn-out valve is all."

I didn't understand why Nana looked so sad when Daddy said that.

"That's all right," she replied after a minute.

Daddy got in the car, and I waved. I waved again as he pulled onto the road, but he wasn't looking.

In the kitchen, Nana smoothed my hair behind my ears and cradled my face in her hands, which smelled of lye soap.

"Just making sure you washed behind your ears," she said. I hugged her, burying my face in the front of her soft old housedress.

Aunty Rose wanted me to hand her clothespins while she hung the sheets on the line, something she could do very well for herself. She had at least one question for every clothespin I put in her hand. I thought about telling her that Grandfather Clark made wine and the whole family drank it but me.

When Grandpa came in at noon, he seemed to wash my hands extra good between his, like he was trying to wash my daddy off. After dinner, we went across the road to see my livestock.

I kind of kept waiting for my daddy to turn up again that day, but he didn't.

What did he mean when he said he'd be back *soon?*

At dusk, I lay on my back in the grass, watching the chimney swallows circle, then drop into the chimney one by one. After the last swallow had disappeared, I gazed into the flat blue sky. The longer I looked, the deeper the sky got, and I could feel the earth moving.

Heaven was up there somewhere. But Nana said it was so high, we couldn't see it from earth. Still, I kept looking. I wouldn't mind catching a glimpse of Mama. I wished I knew what she thought about Daddy's being home.

Daddy didn't turn up the next day, either, which was a Tuesday, and just when I was wondering if it had all been a dream, I heard the sound of the Model A pulling in the drive while I was helping Nana and Aunty Rose with the supper dishes.

Grandpa was over on the south hill where the hen-houses were, fixing the roof of one. I could hear the echo of his hammering.

When Daddy didn't come in the house, I went out and stood beside the dusty Model A.

"Just thought I'd make sure you're still here," he said.

Where else would I be?

"I was thinking about going down to the cemetery," he said. "Wondered if you might like to come along."

Daddy stared at the hills to the east as he asked this, and I got the feeling he thought I might say no. But a cemetery is a lonely place to be by yourself.

I went in the house for Nana, and she walked back to the car with me.

"You won't be gone long, will you?" she asked.

"'Bout an hour," Daddy said.

Panther Fork cemetery was down the road, then a quarter of a mile to the west. We had it all to ourselves except for the preacher's beagle that ambled across the road from the parsonage for a petting.

In the low light, the shadows of the monuments stretched to the east. I could see the tip of the angel's wings just over the hilltop.

Daddy hadn't been home since Mama's marker was put up.

"That's Mama's, over there." I pointed up the hill in the direction we were walking.

The way Daddy stopped breathing for a second told me I should have prepared him better.

"It's mighty fine," he said, after he got used to what he was seeing. "Mighty fine."

It was so quiet in the cemetery, you could practically hear the dead folks remembering. Two squirrels chased along the branch of a big oak tree, and acorns dropped on the path.

When we got to Mama's grave, we just stood. Daddy didn't say anything, but it was like he'd waked Mama up a little by being there. A tear ran down my cheek, and I let the breeze dry it.

Finally Daddy circled Mama's angel, his hands in his pockets, like he was inspecting it for cracks. Then he cupped his hand over my head, and I could feel his fingers trembling.

We walked back down the path, but instead of taking it to the bottom of the hill, Daddy pointed over by the sandstone fence.

"Let's go over there for a minute."

Where was he going? We were getting closer and closer to the grave of the mystery baby. In the lowering light, the little tablet-shaped marker glowed.

Daddy stopped in front of it, and I grabbed my chance. "Is this Mama's baby?"

The words were already out of my mouth before I saw the look on his face. He flicked his gaze from the marker to me.

"You mean you don't know this is your little brother?" he said, his voice hoarse.

My little brother?

Laid out like that, the news did more than answer my question; it made me feel . . . smaller.

I looked at my daddy, shaking my head.

He shook his head right back, his mouth tight and his eyes flat.

Why was my daddy mad at me?

I might as well go ahead and ask all my questions. Things were stirred up enough, they couldn't get much worse.

"If Baby Clark is my brother, why is he buried over here?"

After long enough for a weed to grow an inch, Daddy focused on me. "You'll have to ask Will."

It didn't seem like a good time to tell Daddy I wouldn't dare ask Grandpa, so I just nodded.

We listened to the locusts screech, and I wondered what Daddy was thinking as he stared at my baby brother's grave.

Finally he cleared his throat. "I got some grandparents buried over there. You know that? They'd be your great-grandparents."

"Is their name Clark?" I asked.

"No, it's Melton. Samantha and Harold. I was named for him. Let's go see if they're still there," he said, working a little joke into his voice.

Chapter 6

Daddy started coming around about every day. Sometimes I'd just carry out two glasses of tea and lean against the fender, listening to how his job hunting was going. Nobody wanted him to wire their house. If they were getting electricity, they'd already signed up with the Green boys, who had a fancy truck with their names on it and a business card that said they'd been wiring electricity since 1937.

Other days, I rode with him into Huxley or wherever he was going. And sometimes I'd go down and see Grandmother and Grandfather Clark and Aunt Belle.

But every time Grandpa heard the Model A turn in

the drive, if he was in the house, he'd duck out the side door and disappear to the barn or across the road to the sheep pasture. Likewise, when I got home from visiting the Clarks, sometimes staying for a day or two at a time, Grandpa never made the least mention of my absence.

Nana listened when I talked about things I did with my daddy, like going to the barbershop, then tossing peanuts to the pigeons around the courthouse square. But I could tell she wanted to ease me onto other subjects as soon as it seemed polite.

When Grandpa and Nana weren't around, Aunty Rose rained questions on me about the Clarks and what I did with Daddy. When I turned the questions back on her, though, and asked what made the trouble between the families, her tongue turned to stone.

During this back-and-forth time, the hottest summer on record sat down on southern Illinois like a flatiron straight off the stove. The radio talked about it every day. Old folks dropping down on the streets of Huxley from heatstroke, people getting into fights over nothing, cattle sickening in the heat.

One Tuesday afternoon in early August, I lay on my bed reading the book that Grandfather Clark had given me for my birthday. A breeze through the south windows teased my sweaty legs. The house was quiet as Nana and Aunty Rose and even Grandpa gave up on working during the heat of the day.

I liked all the stories in the birthday book, but I kept coming back to the one of the baby getting carried off by the eagle. I pored over the illustration of the mother climbing the rocks, her face lifted upward, as she went to get her baby back.

"Want to ride down to Lorrimer's with me?"

Grandpa stood in the doorway, crease lines from his nap still on his face.

I smacked the book shut and rolled over on my stomach, hiding it beneath me.

"Sure," I squeaked.

His brows curved in puzzlement, then his face closed as he figured out the book was somehow part of my other life. The only book we had was the Good Book.

I put on my shoes and met Grandpa by the car. As we turned south, we raised a cloud of nose-tickling dust. In the dry sheep pasture, my black-faced lamb nibbled a clump of clover sticking up in the mat of brown grass.

At Lorrimer's, Grandpa went around back to get the

chicken feed and I went inside. The store was empty, smelling of dust and heat. Mrs. Lorrimer hunched over a radio, listening to a ball game.

Although Nana said I should never ask for anything, I asked Mrs. Lorrimer for a chunk of ice from the soda pop cooler.

"Sure, hon, help yourself," she said, glancing up. "The iceman comes tomorrow." She leaned closer to the radio as the announcer's voice rose in excitement.

"All right!" she said, standing up, her freckled face flushed. "You a Cardinals fan?"

"Yes, ma'am," I said. How else could I answer in the face of such generosity?

She nodded. "Well, our man Stan just hit a homer. Almost knocked it out of Sportsman's Park. Isn't that something?"

"Sure is," I said, nearly singing with joy as my arm plunged into the icy cooler water. The bottles rattled against one another as I sloshed around, trying to find a good hunk of ice.

I lifted out one about the size of a muskmelon, though it was some smaller by the time we got home and sat around the well curb, in the shade of the hickory tree, rubbing the ice on our faces and arms.

By the time the chunk had become a marble, Aunty Rose and Nana were laughing, and Grandpa went off to the machine shed whistling.

I crunched the very last sliver of ice between my back teeth and petted Jacky with my toes, wondering what my daddy was doing to stay cool.

❧   ❧   ❧

On Wednesday, Daddy picked me up right after breakfast.

"You a good mechanic?" he asked, turning south.

"I don't think so," I said. "Are you?"

"Yes, ma'am." He pushed back the bill of his cap. "I can fix anything 'cept a broken heart."

Daddy leaned forward, seeming to urge Grandfather Clark's old car to go faster. He was singing under his breath.

Hey, lolly, lolly, lolly. Hey, lolly, lolly lo.

The sky was bright blue, and I put my hand out the window, opening my fingers to let the breeze brush between them.

Daddy sang louder.

I leaned my head back. I didn't know anybody who sang as fine. Even singers on the radio had people helping them—playing the piano or filling in the background. But Daddy did it all by himself. He just opened his mouth and music came dancing out.

"Sing with me," he said, raising his chest up for an even louder chorus.

I shook my head.

"Why not?"

I shrugged. "I can't make music."

He looked at me, his flecked eyes determined.

"Sure, you can."

"No, I can't."

He hit a pothole and had to turn his attention back to the road.

"Try," he said after a minute, reaching over and touching my arm. "Just sing the first four words."

To please him, I opened my mouth and put the words *Hey, lolly, lolly, lolly* out in the air.

Suddenly the sun didn't seem as bright.

The lines around Daddy's eyes said he noticed it too.

"Well," he said, shifting gears. "You make me want to sing, so you can be my inspiration. How's that?"

"That's good," I said. "That's the best way to do it."

After we turned east, he sang about Ezekiel's wheel

until we bounced up the driveway at Grandmother and Grandfather Clark's house. In my heart, I sang with him, proud of my red-haired, skinny daddy with magic in his voice.

We parked under a crab apple tree next to a shed with peeling paint.

"Our mechanical project is in here," Daddy said.

When he rolled open the door, sunlight fell on the rear end of a car, heavy with dust, cobwebs, and bird poop.

"Well, there she is."

"That car's a mess, Daddy," I said, sneezing from the dust he raised as he walked around to the front. "Does it run?"

"Nope." Daddy sounded almost happy about it.

"How long has it been in there?"

"Since before the war." He'd disappeared into the shadows, then the car rolled a few inches backward. "Reckon you can steer," he asked, "while I push it into the shade?"

Grandpa sometimes let me sit close to him and steer the Packard if there wasn't anybody coming.

"I'll try," I said.

Daddy had to show me how to cut the wheel so the car went into the shade as he pushed.

I couldn't see through the filthy windows, so I just had to do what he told me.

When I got out, I saw that the old car was even a worse mess in the light. The fenders were so rusted, they looked like brown lace.

"What happened to the fenders?" I asked, knocking a clump of bird poop off with a corncob.

"Grasshoppers ate 'em back in '36. Grasshoppers were pretty near starving that year. You ever hear about that?"

"I never did," I said, not letting on to his tease. "Want me to start chipping the dirt daubers' nests off?"

"That'd be good," he said.

Daddy stripped off his shirt, propped up the hood, and bent over the engine.

Pretty soon, sweat stained his undershirt and his dungarees blossomed with grease spots.

My hands and clothes were filthy from leaning against the car to attack the dried mud tunnels left by the dirt daubers.

Aunt Belle brought us out a jug of tea about midmorning, and I went back to the house with her to wash my hands at the washstand on the back porch.

Inside, Grandmother Clark offered me a piece of

bread and strawberry jelly and asked me if I didn't want to stay inside a while.

"I think I'll take a jelly sandwich over to Daddy," I said.

So we slathered the red jelly onto a piece of bread and I went back to where Daddy was working.

"Got you a jelly sandwich," I said to his back.

He straightened up from where he'd been bent over the engine. His eyes lit up at the sight of the strawberry jelly.

"Here," I offered, holding the piece of bread out.

He looked at his hands, which were black. He had grease streaks on his face and down the front of his grimy undershirt.

"Fold it up and I can eat it in three bites," he instructed, opening his mouth.

He ended up with jelly on his nose.

"I've never been this dirty in my life," I declared, wiping my sticky hands on my shorts. "It's kind of fun."

We went in for lunch, but otherwise we worked all afternoon.

I gave up trying to clean the outside of the car and helped Daddy take the engine apart. He handed me pieces of metal—bolts and wing nuts and shafts—that I rinsed in gasoline, then scrubbed with an old toothbrush.

Eventually the black grease came out of the cracks, and I laid the gleaming pieces on a blanket.

"Do I need to keep these in any special order, Daddy?"

"Nah. I know where they all go."

"You sure?"

"Yep," he said, seating a socket wrench over a nut.

We worked at taking the engine apart on Wednesday and Thursday. Then on Friday and Saturday, we put it back together, making a trip to Huxley once for spark plugs and a belt. I went home every night, and Aunty Rose said I smelled like a grease monkey, and Grandpa looked closely at my hands as we washed together.

I could tell by his stiffness that he didn't like what he saw. Grandpa wasn't mechanical, and when something needed to be fixed, he had one of Uncle Retus's boys come down, or he took it to a mechanic in town.

One night, I heard Nana rearing through the wall. ". . . Seems like he'd have more sense than to let a girl get in the grease."

❧ ❧ ❧

Sunday morning, Nana had to take a brush and lye soap to my hands to make them presentable for church.

"Are you mad at me, Nana?" I asked as she bent over my hands, scrubbing around my fingernails.

She looked up. "No, I'm not mad at you."

"Then are you mad at my daddy?"

She sighed. "He just doesn't show good sense," she said.

After church, like always, I set the table with our Sunday dishes while Nana fried chicken and Aunty Rose got ready to go out with Charles Michael and their friends.

Grandpa was in his rocker in the sunroom, reading the New Testament.

After I'd put the silverware around, I went in the sunroom and leaned against Grandpa's arm.

He sat up straighter and made a place for me to sit on his knee, which I hadn't done for a long time. He laid the Bible down.

"My daddy has been home for a month now," I said, settling on his knee.

Grandpa's granite blue eyes met mine, and for a minute, I thought he was going to ignore my conversation. Then he nodded. Not a very big nod—but enough to say he'd heard me.

"I guess we're just going to have to get used to it," I stated after a while.

Grandpa looked away, staring at the wall calendar like he'd never seen a picture of a waterfall before. Then he looked back at me.

"I reckon," he said with a sigh.

My heart lightened. I leaned forward and gave him a quick hug, then ran to help Nana take up the dinner.

❧   ❧   ❧

On Monday, I didn't even hear the car. I just heard Daddy's voice calling "Anybody home?" through the screen door to the kitchen.

Grandpa was in the field, Aunty Rose was upstairs cleaning out her wardrobe, and Nana was over at Uncle Retus's, helping wallpaper the kitchen.

"Did you walk?" I asked, holding the screen open for him.

"Why would I walk when I got a good car?" he said, bouncing on the balls of his feet. "You better come see."

Daddy had washed and waxed the old car until it gleamed. Except for the rusted places, it looked beautiful. I circled it, remembering what a mess it had been when he rolled it out of the shed.

"Does it run right?" I asked.

He shrugged. "Runs as good as it's ever going to run

102

again. Doesn't run like a new car, of course. But it's fifteen years old. You want to go for a ride? Try it out? Since you helped with the work."

"Sure," I said. "Can Aunty Rose come?"

"That would be fine."

Aunty Rose pulled on a clean blouse and brushed her hair. She brushed mine too and clipped in barrettes. We wrote Nana a note, saying we were out riding with my daddy.

Aunty Rose sat in the back, and we rolled down all the windows. Daddy drove as fast as he could on the rough roads, showing off the car.

"Daddy took it all apart," I told Aunty Rose. "Every little bit and piece, and fixed it."

"You helped," Daddy said.

I looked over the backseat at Aunty Rose. She was frowning.

"Willa Mae's a girl, Harold. Treva wouldn't want her fixing cars."

A line of red moved up Daddy's neck. He opened his mouth, then shut it.

"Wish you had a radio," Aunty Rose said. "Charles Michael's car has a radio."

"Daddy doesn't need a radio," I said. "He can sing."

We rode in silence for a while, and I was thinking it would have been more fun without Aunty Rose.

"Maybe you could get a job as a mechanic someplace, Harold," Aunty Rose said, by way of making up. "Good mechanics are hard to find, I hear."

"I've looked into it. But nobody needs a mechanic right now. Not around here, at least. And I've still got my mind set on wiring houses, being an electrician."

"Maybe you could work for the Greens," she said. "They're the ones who do all the wiring."

"I don't want to work for the Greens."

When we got back to the house, Aunty Rose thanked Daddy for the ride and ran in to start dinner.

Daddy got out of the car and we stood leaning against the fender.

"I may not be by for a few days, Mae Bug," he said, putting his arm around my shoulders.

"How come?"

"I'm going to Vincennes, Indiana, to an army surplus auction."

"What for?" I asked.

"Well, I might sell this car and buy a truck," he said. "If it works out. And if I do buy a truck," he added, "I might have to do some work on it before I drive it home."

That was a lot of "mights," but I thought I saw where Daddy was leading. If he had a truck, he could get a sign painted on it just like the Green boys, then he could give them a run for their money. But it seemed like bad luck to talk about it, so I just said okay, I'd see him when he got back.

Chapter 7

Mid-August was peach-canning time. So the next few days, while Daddy was away, we worked on the peaches.

Every morning, as soon as it was light enough to see the fruit, we drove down to Neidermeyer's Orchard. We picked two bushels each day—Grandpa going up the ladder and handing the fruit down to us. Nana fussed at Aunty Rose and me not to bruise the peaches as we laid them in baskets, but my arms itched so much from the fuzz, I could hardly wait to be done.

At home, Nana peeled and pitted and sliced, and Aunty Rose boiled the simple syrup to pour over the fruit.

My job was to lug up boxes of empty mason jars from the basement. The boxes were powdery with dust, and some of the quart jars had dried-up spiders and moths in them.

Because my hands were still small enough to fit through the necks, I drew dish-washing duty, and my fingers stung from the hot, soapy water.

The heat of the stove and the steam of the pressure cooker made the sweat pour off all of us. The only relief came from the sweet slices of peaches Nana slipped in our mouths right off the knife tip.

On Wednesday, after two days of my being home all the time, Grandpa said at the dinner table, "Reckon your daddy has skipped the country?"

I blinked.

The sun seemed to pass from behind a cloud.

"He's just gone to Indiana to an auction," I explained.

"An auction," Grandpa said, sounding disappointed and critical at the same time.

I guess Grandpa was kind of hoping Daddy had gone away for good.

On Thursday, about dark, we were sitting at the table eating a light supper of corn bread and milk and listening to the radio when Daddy came up on the side porch.

This time, Grandpa didn't get up to leave, and hope sang in my heart that they might make up.

"Come in, Harold," Nana said, switching off the radio.

I stood up, glad Daddy had come at supper time. Would Grandpa let him sit down at the table with us?

"Willa Mae says you've been to an auction."

I caught my breath, holding it, praying they'd talk to each other.

"Did you get a truck?" I asked, encouraging Daddy.

"Yes, I got a truck," he said, something warning me in his voice.

The hair stood right up on my arms. Nana sensed something too and reached over and laid her hand on top of mine.

"My brother, Les, thinks I can get work wiring in Oklahoma," Daddy said. "And he's found us a place to live. So we'll be leaving in the morning, Mae Bug. First thing."

I shook my head, imagining I'd heard Daddy tell us he was taking me away. Then the oak back of Grandpa's chair cracked as it hit the floor. He stood, seeming about twice as big as Daddy. Grandpa strode through the kitchen, slamming the back door behind him.

The rest of us sat in our chairs.

I waited, hoping any minute I was going to wake up and see the rosebud wallpaper on my bedroom wall instead of Daddy standing in the kitchen, talking crazy.

Aunty Rose spoke first.

"You can't do that," she said, standing up. "You can't take Willa Mae. She's ours."

Daddy shook his head back and forth, his mouth set.

I just stared at him.

"I'll be here at sunup," he said. "You be ready to go, Willa Mae."

Willa Mae? He hardly ever called me Willa Mae. I gripped the seat of my chair.

Aunty Rose threw her spoon at him, splashing milk all over the door frame where it hit.

"Rose!" Nana stood up.

Daddy turned on his heel and was out the door before my tears came. I twined my legs through the rungs of my chair and clung to Nana, who'd come to stand beside me.

She talked, rubbing my back, saying words I didn't want to hear. Finally, Aunty Rose led me upstairs, and I lay on her bed, my face buried in my arms, crying. Aunty Rose sat beside me, fiddling with my hair. After what seemed like forever, I got up and went to the window. Against the lantern light in the barn, Grandpa's silhouette moved back and forth, back and forth, like a panther pacing.

Maybe he was fixing up a place to hide me. A place where my daddy would never think to look, so he'd have to go to Oklahoma alone.

Aunty Rose had pulled on her old ruffled blue nightgown and sat at the dressing table. Turning up the lamp, she blew her nose, then began to brush her hair three hundred times.

I lifted my own hair off my sweaty neck and used some of Aunty Rose's bobby pins to hold it up.

"Can I sleep with you tonight?" I asked, my voice not working very well. How could I spend the last night in my own bed?

She put her arms around me, and I felt her nodding.

Later, as we lay side by side on top of the sheets, moonlight cutting across our bare legs, Aunty Rose stared at the shadows of the tree leaves on the wall.

For a long time, I listened to the sounds of Nana's moving around. She said she was going to send some canned goods to Oklahoma with us. She said my daddy wasn't a bad man. She said he sprung the news on me fast because he thought it would hurt less. She said somehow they'd get along without me. She said everything would be okay by and by. She said he was my daddy, and a child needed a daddy.

But when would I see Nana again? How far was Oklahoma? If Uncle Les had gone there before the war and never come home, would I ever get home? Did my daddy know how to cook? What would I do when I outgrew my clothes? Who would take care of me when I got sick? How could I live without Nana? How could I grow up without Aunty Rose to show me the way? What kind of people lived in Oklahoma? Would they like me?

My head ached from questions and tears.

Grandpa finally came in about midnight, when the clock at the foot of the stairs had just finished bonging twelve times, and I heard voices in the kitchen, but I couldn't make out what they were saying.

In the morning, I tried not to feel Aunty Rose jostling me. I wanted to crawl back in the deep, warm nest of her arms and her pillows and stay there forever.

"Mom's calling," she whispered.

I swung my legs off the bed, tugging at my nightgown. Pale light lit the room, and birds in the hickory tree made a din.

Nana waited at the foot of the stairs. I stood in front of her, not able to meet her eyes.

She touched my shoulder. "Did you sleep?" she asked. I nodded.

"Well." She cleared her throat. "I put two mason jar boxes in your room. For you to pack your things in. Best pack all your clothes, even if they're dirty."

I turned away.

In my room, I pulled clean underpants, slips, socks, and my birthday pajamas out of my drawers, then two pairs of shorts Nana had made, with blouses to match. I put those in one of the boxes. Then I folded up my hanging clothes—one Sunday dress, a dress to wear to town, and two everyday dresses that almost didn't fit anymore. I laid those on top and tucked in the flaps of the box.

Into the other box, I dropped my Sunday shoes and the old pillowcase holding my dirty clothes. I tucked in the book of stories Grandfather Clark had given me and my hairbrush and toothbrush.

Then I stripped off my gown and pulled on a pair of blue shorts and a white sailor blouse, a pair of white anklets and my saddle oxfords.

Aunty Rose came in, standing in the doorway, her face swollen and her gown rumpled.

I thought she might try to hug me, and I didn't want

her to because if I started crying, I might just keep on until I'd swamped the farm and drowned the chickens and washed away the pigs and sheep.

"Excuse me," I said, picking up a box and staring into space until she stepped aside.

I carried my boxes out to the well curb and waited there, wishing my daddy would hurry so the pain of saying good-bye to Nana and Grandpa and Aunty Rose could be over with.

Grandpa made his way from the barn, carrying a bucket sloshing with Old Jerse's milk, and set it down. He'd done this every morning of my life, and he'd do it tomorrow morning. But I wouldn't be here.

I turned my face away, but I could still hear him rolling up his sleeves and pumping a pan of water for washing. And I smelled the cheesy warmth of Old Jerse's milk.

"Need to wash?" he asked. "So you can have a bite of breakfast before you get on the road?"

I shook my head, keeping it turned away, not letting him see the tears trickling down my cheeks.

"I reckon you and your daddy will have some adventures," Grandpa said, making splashing noises. "Won't you come in for a bite of breakfast?" he asked one more time.

I shook my head again, my throat aching from trying to dam up tears.

When I heard the screen door finally bounce shut behind Grandpa, I called Jacky. He came, blowing his hot, damp breath in my face, whining.

"You won't forget me, will you?" I whispered, tears running down my neck.

Daddy pulled in just then, and I brushed my eyes with my fingers. The truck was bigger than I'd expected. The rising sun silhouetted it, black and square. He'd not got anything painted on the door like the Green boys, but the truck sure looked like it could belong to an electrician. It groaned as Daddy shifted into low and pulled up under the hickory tree. He cut the engine and climbed out.

Despite myself, I walked out to look, trying to imagine riding hundreds of miles in it.

Daddy opened the back, and I looked in at his metal toolbox and some packages wrapped in paper and tied with string.

For sure, if the truck broke down on the road to Oklahoma, he would fix it. I didn't have to worry about that.

Nana and Grandpa and Aunty Rose came out. Nana kept hugging her arms as if she were cold. Everybody was very polite to one another. The truck bed rocked as Daddy worked in the back, loading the food that Nana was sending with us—quart jars of blackberries, peaches, beans, and corn. Pints of apple butter and grape jelly.

"Thanks, Mae. I'm not much of a cook."

I saw the look on Nana's face when he said that.

"But don't worry," he said, realizing his mistake. "I won't let her starve."

Finally he climbed behind the wheel.

The time had come.

Aunty Rose, wrapped in her blue chenille robe, blew her nose.

I stepped up on the running board, then into the cab, surprised at how high I sat. It must be kind of like riding a camel.

"You have a safe trip," Grandpa said. I felt his eyes on my face, and I finally looked at him.

"Take care of my livestock?" I asked, surprised I could make my lips move.

He nodded. "I sure will."

He looked at me a while longer, like he might be trying to say something else. Then he turned and headed toward the barn.

Nana leaned in and brushed my hair behind my ear.

"Don't worry," she said. "Your daddy will take good care of you."

I glanced at Daddy when she said that, and I saw his Adam's apple bob.

I could smell the garden on Nana's hands, and the soap she washed with.

I held my breath, trying not to start crying again.

Then Aunty Rose leaned in the window and I threw my arms around her neck, breathing in the smell of her hair like it was the last bit of oxygen in the world.

"Write to me every day," she whispered. "And I'll write you."

I nodded. *Every day*, I thought, but I couldn't make the words come out. Finally she had to loosen my arms. Daddy leaned across me and pulled the door shut.

Aunty Rose and Nana and I waved at each other until they vanished behind the stand of evergreens south of the house. Then I dropped my hands in my lap and stared through the windshield. The blue sky, with only two little streaky clouds in it, looked big and empty.

116

Chapter 8

The world looked different from so high up.

"They sure are going to miss me when school starts," I said as Panther Fork School came into view on the left side of the road.

Maybe it wasn't too late to change Daddy's mind.

A bare flagpole stuck up out of the unmowed grass, and dust and flyspecks dulled the windows.

"Mrs. Henry won't have an even dozen anymore without me," I added.

But Daddy watched the road, his left arm straight on the steering wheel as if pointing the way to Oklahoma. "There'll be other new kids starting that school," he offered.

Well, sure, one of the little Miller kids would probably turn six, but that wasn't the point.

"You went to school there, Daddy," I said. "And so did Mama."

I watched his profile, hopeful for a sign that he might turn around and take me back.

For a minute, he slowed and stopped, and I thought I'd won. But he was just leaning on the steering wheel to have one last look at Panther Fork School. Then he gave the truck some gas and we went on.

Up this high, I could see little sparkles of water among the roots of the ditch grass.

"Times are changing, Mae Bug," he said. "People don't stay in the same place where they were born the way they used to. Look at Les. He moved off."

"But—"

"And I can't find us a place to live around here," he continued. "And so far, I've not been able to find work. All the servicemen who beat me home got to the jobs and houses first."

"But *I* could stay here," I said, trying to be reasonable. "Just until things get settled."

His jaw tightened, and he shifted gears, going faster

despite the rough roads. I heard Nana's canned goods clinking in the back.

We bounced along through the countryside and I took stock of the things I wouldn't be seeing for a while.

"How long are we going to stay away, Daddy?" I asked.

He shook his head, looking around at the familiar places too. "I don't know, Willa Mae. I've got to make a living. And provide a home for you."

The road smoothed out as we moved away from the rural electrification work. But when we bounced over the railroad tracks in Mills, Nana's canned goods clanked in the back again.

Just a few miles past Mills, we came to the highway. Going north, it went to Huxley. Going south, the way we turned, it went to the very edge of the earth for all I knew— though I guess Oklahoma was somewhere along the way.

"You know where we're going, Daddy?" I asked.

"We're going to head down to Chester and cross the river there."

"What river?" I said, thinking of Panther Creek and the water moccasin Grandpa had caught.

"Why, the Mississippi River," Daddy said. "The one that divides Illinois from Missouri."

"The Mississippi River?"

Daddy glanced at me.

"The one and only," he answered, the sun coming out on his face as he heard my wonder.

"But I don't know anybody my age who has crossed the Mississippi River," I said.

In school, we studied about the great river, the bold blue line down through the continent of North America. But that line seemed no more related to our lives than the pictures of the Taj Mahal and the Leaning Tower of Pisa. Yet here I was, going to cross it this very day! So that's what Grandpa had meant about adventures.

What was Grandpa doing right now? And Nana and Aunty Rose? I saw them in my mind, going about the morning chores, but I wasn't in the picture. A hole of emptiness burned inside me, and I put my hands over my stomach.

Daddy looked at me. "You okay?"

I nodded.

"Just excited?"

I looked at Daddy. His face shone with so much hope that I nodded again.

The countryside wasn't much different from the farms

and little towns around home as we drove southwest through Illinois.

"I want to get there by tomorrow night," he told me, turning his head from side to side to work the tiredness out of his shoulders.

"Where are we going to live?"

"Les has found us a furnished apartment. It's upstairs in the landlady's house. He says it's pretty big."

Daddy glanced at me again, his eyes searching for interest on my part.

I had never been in an apartment. I shut my eyes, thinking of our house at the farm and trying to imagine living in the upstairs.

The warm air blowing up through the floor vents and the humming of the truck tires on the highway lulled me. Soon images of our furnished apartment in Oklahoma got mixed up with Nana's dressmaker's dummy in the upstairs storage room at home.

I jerked awake with a start.

Daddy was singing snatches of a song under his breath about a gypsy.

"You won't fall asleep and run off the road, will you, Daddy?"

"Hope not."

"Sing louder," I said. "So I know you're awake."

Daddy laughed, curling his fingers around my arm, the reddish hairs on his hands gleaming in the light. Daddy had square hands, like mine.

I held my hand out in front of me.

"What are you looking at?" Daddy said.

"Our hands are shaped alike," I said. "But I can't sing."

Daddy stared ahead, and I thought he'd forgotten what I'd asked him to do. But I guess he was just finding the rhythm in the road, because soon he started low and built up, the sad story of the little blue-eyed girl who lost her mama to the wandering gypsy Davy.

It was late last night when the boss came home,
He was asking about his lady.
The only answer he received
Was she's gone with the gypsy Davy,
Gone with the gypsy Dave.

When the man goes looking for his wife, he finds her sitting around the campfire, happy with the singing gypsy.

Daddy's voice pleaded when he sang:

Have you forsaken your house and home?
Have you forsaken your baby?
Have you forsaken your husband dear?
To go with the gypsy Davy
And sing with the gypsy Dave?

The mother is happy to forsake him, but she weeps at leaving her daughter.

Daddy sang about the husband begging her:

Take off, take off your buckskin gloves
Made of Spanish leather.
Give to me your lily-white hand,
And we'll ride back home together.

I hoped she'd go with her husband, back home where she belonged. I looked at my hand again, trying to imagine it in Spanish leather. How could the mama not go home to her baby?

But Daddy sang of her resolve to follow the gypsy.

No, I won't take off my buckskin gloves.
They're made of Spanish leather.
I'll go my way from day to day
And sing with the gypsy Davy,

That song of the gypsy Dave.
That song of the gypsy Davy,
That song of the gypsy Dave.

I stayed awake most of the night, feeling safe as long as Daddy was singing. I rested my head on his leg, feeling it move as he clutched and accelerated, and listened to the story over and over of the mama who left her baby. Thank goodness the daddy was still there.

I must have fallen asleep again, because Daddy's hand on my head woke me up.

"We're coming to the river."

I heard the excitement in his voice and pushed myself up, my head feeling like it had been stuffed with cotton wool.

Daddy's green work shirt showed dark sweat stains across his back as he stretched forward over the steering wheel.

"About to go to sleep myself," he said. "You want to drive when we get across the river?"

I tried to grin, but my lips were stuck together with the dryness of sleep. The air from the floor vent rushed against my legs, drying the sweat.

The bridge surface sang beneath the truck's tires and struts of the bridge flashed by.

I sat on my knees and put my head out the open window. "Slow down, Daddy," I said.

How could a river be so wide? It glinted steely gray, like metal, strong with its size. Tiny whitecaps crossed its currents in drifting triangles. A gull, bluish white, swooped between the struts of the bridge.

Daddy crept along, letting me watch the barges and tugboats until a car came up on our tail.

"Did you know it's the biggest river on the North American continent?" I asked, sitting back in the seat. "We learned that in school."

"Yep," Daddy said, staring just as much as I was at the water traffic passing right under us.

"Have you seen this river before, Daddy?"

He nodded. "Several times."

The air floating through the truck cab smelled of the river.

When we came off the bridge on the other side of the water, in a whole other state, I said, "Wait until I tell them at school!"—forgetful for a second that I wouldn't be going there.

Daddy glanced at me. "Do you reckon you'll do okay in a big town school?" he asked.

"A big town school?"

I'd thought about where I wouldn't be. I hadn't thought about where I *would* be.

"I probably won't be the only sixth grader," I said.

Daddy shook his head, and I saw a shadow of concern.

"Did you ever go to a town school?" I asked.

"Not until high school. And then it wasn't very big."

"Will they have more books in a big town school?"

He shrugged. "It stands to reason that they would. More pupils should mean more books."

I thought of the storybook from Grandfather Clark in my box in the back of the truck. I'd like to read many more books like that.

"Town school might be okay," I said after a while.

Daddy seemed to relax. He shifted gears and the truck growled as we began the long climb out of the river valley.

"You hungry?" he asked.

"What time is it?"

"Time to eat. Your grandma sent us enough grub to feed the navy."

In a few more miles, Daddy pulled into the tall grass at the side of the road and stopped. A couple of small farmsteads, with red outbuildings, lay in valleys of low hills.

"Want to stretch your legs?" Daddy asked.

I'd forgotten what my feet felt like, and I staggered as I slid off the high seat to the ground. I walked into the field, each step sending up a spray of grasshoppers.

A cloudless hazy sky capped the Missouri hills.

When a cow bawled in the distance, making me remember Old Jerse, I thought I'd just die of homesickness right there in the grass.

But the wave of homesickness passed, and I felt so hungry, there might have been a pinching bug running around inside my stomach.

"Did Nana send biscuits?" I yelled back to Daddy, who was opening up the back of the truck.

He handed out a white box. When I opened it, all the biscuits left from breakfast, sliced and filled with bacon, made my mouth water.

We spooned peaches out of a quart jar and shared the sandwiches, then we got back on the road.

We drove through hilly country, with houses and little towns hugging the hillsides like the thumb of God had pressed them in. We read so many Burma Shave signs, Daddy said they were making his whiskers grow. Seemed like every hundred yards we'd see another clothesline of pretty chenille bedspreads with peacocks and butterflies in bright colors for sale. But all the road signs telling about this and that sometimes made it hard to see the bedspreads.

About midafternoon we got in the middle of an army convoy, and going up and down the hills became a lot slower.

"How much longer, Daddy?" I finally asked once we saw the sign saying Welcome to Oklahoma.

"Depends. If we could get out of this army convoy, we could drive faster."

But when we got past one army truck, another just took its place, and the afternoon went by.

Finally we got rid of the convoy, but then the road curved so much, we seemed to be going more sideways than forward.

Daddy started singing, *The Cumberland Gap, the Cumberland Gap, seventeen miles to the Cumberland Gap*. When the road curved, he'd sing, *Nineteen miles to the Cumberland Gap*.

I hated thinking we were getting farther away from where we were going and wished we were like the gulls we had seen on the river and could fly straight over the hills. But Daddy's music at least made the minutes go faster.

By the time we got to the town where Uncle Les lived, and where we were going to live, the low sun cast long shadows. The country looked red, like places I'd seen in western movies with Nana and Grandpa on Saturday night.

I put on my shoes as we drove past the square with a big sandstone courthouse sheltered by giant elms. The businesses lining the square made me think of Huxley.

Then I saw the school, a fire escape coming out of the third floor like a giant covered sliding board.

"Look, Daddy," I said, pointing.

But he was thinking about street names. "You see Linden anyplace?" he asked.

"There," I said, a minute later.

And in no time, we'd found the address Uncle Les had sent Daddy and parked the truck in front. A landlady, who acted like she knew she'd made a mistake renting to us, led us up a dark, creaky staircase. We stood in the middle of a dim, almost empty room that stunk of mothballs and dust. Nana would have had her rags and cleaning bucket out in a second.

"I thought you said Uncle Lesley had found us a furnished apartment, Daddy," I said as soon as Mrs. Stanton, the landlady, had shut the door behind herself. My voice echoed. "How come there's one bed, a little old card table, two folding chairs, and that's all?"

Daddy sounded tired and disappointed too. "Well, this is Oklahoma, Mae Bug. Times haven't caught up with the war being over yet, I guess."

"Harold Clark."

We turned toward the door, and in walked a tall blue-eyed giraffe of a man in fancy boots, holding a cowboy hat to his stomach.

"Lesley Clark." Daddy crossed the room in two strides and took Uncle Les by the hand, pumping his arm up and down.

Uncle Lesley pounded Daddy on the back, then hugged him.

"And who's this?" he asked, bending down and looking at me at eye level.

"I'm Willa Mae Clark," I said, fighting off the urge to giggle, then putting out my hand.

The giraffe clasped it. "I'm your uncle Lesley Clark. Pleased to meet you, kitten.

"Saw the truck go by my place of business when you drove through town," he said to Daddy. "Came to help you unload."

They talked a while about Grandmother and Grandfather Clark and Aunt Belle and how good it was for Daddy to be home after all those years, then they went back to the truck to get our boxes.

Meanwhile I stood in the middle of the room, staring at the cracked, worn green linoleum. How could I live in this awful place? I'd bet there were cockroaches.

Daddy and Uncle Lesley thudded up the stairs, and when Uncle Lesley came through the door, the room exploded with light.

I squeaked, then felt my face flaming with embarrassment.

"Fooled you, huh?" Uncle Lesley said, laughing. "Pretty little country girl who's not used to electric lights."

I gazed around. With Uncle Lesley and the lights, the place didn't seem quite so bad. Or maybe the lights made it seem worse. The lights showed the water stains on the walls and the grime ground into the cracks.

While Daddy and Uncle Les made the second trip, I toured the apartment, flipping on lights. I'd never done such a thing before, and I felt a God-like power. *Let there be light.* Just wait until I told them back home.

But then I discovered something even more wonderful than electric lights.

"Daddy, come here!" I yelled, hearing their footsteps on the stairs. "Look!" I pointed to the little room I'd found in the back of the apartment. "Look!"

A claw-footed bathtub stood below a window on the back wall.

"And look, Daddy. There's a pot and basin and everything. Faucets and running water. Drain holes. It's a bathroom, Daddy. Just like in town. Just like in the movies."

Daddy grinned. "The expression on your face is worth a dollar," he said. "Is it better than the Mississippi?"

"Can I take a bath?" I said, not wanting to take time debating the wonders of the world.

"Right now?"

"Right this very minute."

"Why not? Les and I'll finish unloading, then we'll think about supper. Sure. You go ahead and have a bath."

I'd never done this before. But I didn't need anybody to draw pictures for me. I just yanked off my clothes and got in the tub and plugged up the hole and let the water run.

Running the cool water until it was clear up to my armpits, I leaned back and slid all the way under. Then I sat up, shaking my head. My private pond—with no water moccasins. My private swimming pool. Aunty Rose would be green when I wrote her about the bathtub.

The last tenant had left a sliver of soap, cracked and dry, which I worked a little lather out of. Then I lay back in the water again, up to my nostrils, like a spoiled hippo in Africa.

"You learning to swim in there?" Daddy called through the closed door.

I drained the tub and wrung out my hair. "I could," I said. "I got it deep enough."

"Well, Les wants to show us around town."

"I'm coming."

I patted myself dry with my clothes and pulled them back on.

"Who's that looks and smells like flowers after a rain?" Uncle Les asked when I climbed in his pickup.

By this time, darkness had fallen, but the streetlights and the houses glowing with electricity made the night seem almost like day.

"This is my place of business," Uncle Lesley said, stopping in front of a store near the square. Lesley Clark's Sales the sign painted on the big plate glass window said.

He tooted the horn, and the pretty red-haired woman inside, wearing a green dress with polka dots, smiled and waved.

"That a friend of yours?" Daddy asked Uncle Les.

Uncle Les grinned. "You might say."

"I'm hungry," I said when we had been around the square twice and through town both ways. "When will we fix supper, Daddy?"

Uncle Les threw back his head and laughed, and Daddy got a funny look on his face.

"Mae Bug, we've not got any pots and pans to cook with, and we've eaten all the ready-made food your grandma sent. Maybe Les knows where there's a café. Tomorrow we'll set up housekeeping."

After our supper in a café on the square, Uncle Les took us back to the apartment, and Daddy and I set about making the place ready to sleep in. We used some quilts and blankets Mrs. Stanton brought up to make me a pallet beside the bed.

Eventually, from the hard, musty-smelling floor, my stomach churning from the spicy food, I stared out the window of our "furnished" apartment. Then I stared at the cracked, water-marked ceiling. Would the plaster come crashing down in the night and land right on me?

I said my bedtime prayer. *Now I lay me down to sleep.*

I pray the Lord my soul to keep. If I should die before I wake, I pray the Lord my soul to take. Amen.

I worried about the plaster for a while, but at least I had made arrangements with God.

But how could I sleep with streetlights making the room glow practically as bright as day? And about a million cars and trucks going by down below? Without a bed? So far from home?

"Daddy, you asleep?" I whispered.

"No," he whispered back. "You?"

"Yes, I've been asleep for a long time."

"Good," he whispered.

"Let's hold hands," I said. "Every night when we go to bed."

I knew a family needed traditions, like eating mashed potatoes out of the same bowl every Sunday, and this could be Daddy's tradition and mine. It wasn't much, but it would help.

Chapter 9

The next morning, I filled the bathtub before Daddy woke up. The water rose over my ankles, then my knees, and up to my waist. I remembered an illustration in the book that Grandfather Clark had given me of children diving off a giant bar of white soap, swimming under it, lazing on its snowy surface.

Twiddling the ever smaller sliver of old, green soap, I wondered what Aunty Rose was doing right now.

Since it was Saturday, she was probably racing to get all the sweeping done so she could go to Lorrimer's with Nana and Grandpa.

Now that I was gone, who would do the Saturday dusting?

Lowering myself under the water and making bubbles with my breath, I tried not to think about it.

Finally I got out and dried off on my dirty underwear, wondering when Daddy was planning to get us some towels. I pulled an everyday dress over my head and opened the door.

"I've been standing in this line till my feet have gone flat," Daddy teased. "Is there any water left?"

"We need towels," I said, my voice sounding as cross as I felt. "My hair's dripping down my back and my dress is getting all wet."

Daddy looked at me for a long minute. "I've got an idea. Stay right there and shut your eyes."

I hated the feel of the water trickling behind my ear, down my neck and back, not stopping until it hit the elastic waist of my underpants.

Daddy rustled around in the other room. "Keep your eyes shut," he called.

I pressed my arm to my side to blot the water. What was he doing?

When he came back, I felt something soft and clean-smelling press against my head. Daddy squeezed the water out of my hair, then he began to rub, moving the cloth over my scalp.

"Keep your eyes shut," he said again. "Pretend you're the princess in one of those stories Grandfather used to read to you. And I'm your slave. And I'll dry your hair. I may not know how to sew or do fancy cooking like your Nana, but I can dry hair real good."

That was the truth. Nobody had ever dried my hair like this before, taking longer than necessary. My neck relaxed and I turned my head over to his hands.

"What are we having for breakfast?" I asked when he finally stepped back and I opened my eyes, seeing one of his white undershirts in his hand.

"How about we go to that café again? Then we'll see about getting some kitchen supplies."

He spread the shirt over the sunny windowsill to dry. "That can be your special hair-drying cloth," he said. "We won't use it for anything else."

By the time Daddy shaved and we walked downtown, my hair was completely dry. We ordered bacon and eggs, which didn't seem fulfilling without Nana's biscuits and gravy, and Daddy downed three cups of coffee. Then we drove to Uncle Lesley's store.

The red-haired pretty woman I'd seen through the window the night before greeted us.

"Les told me you might stop by," she said, shaking

hands with my daddy. She winked at me, nice and friendly under all that rouge and nail polish.

"I'm Margaret McKenna, according to my birth certificate. But everybody calls me Red. Les went to Arkansas last night, Harold, but he said if you'd take the Wilsons that refrigerator that's out in back, he'll pay you a delivery fee."

While she drew a map, showing Daddy how to get to the Wilsons', I looked around. The store was mainly empty. A saddle hung over a sawhorse in one corner, and a glass case displayed pocketknives. A large sign in the front window said Appliances for Sale, but I didn't see any.

A cash register, a telephone, and a rack of postcards, which I looked through while Miss McKenna finished Daddy's map, covered a small counter.

Daddy drove around back and worked on loading the refrigerator into the truck, and I talked to Miss McKenna—or "Red" as she insisted on being called. She wasn't a whole lot older than Aunty Rose, but she seemed a lot more worldly. I wondered how she kept her fingernails so smooth and shiny.

"You found a boyfriend in this town yet?" she asked me as she sorted through some invoices.

"No." I blushed with embarrassment at her smile.

"Well, you will, with that hair," she said. She tapped

the invoices against the countertop, lining them up. "Look there," she said, watching through the plate glass window. "It's the Norman family, and I'll bet they've come to get that new iron I've been hoarding."

A family that could have been my very own came in the door—the man tall, in clean overalls, the woman soft and blanket-smooth around the edges like Nana. They had a boy about my age and an older girl with them.

Red sent me to the storage room in the back to get the iron.

The smell of newly sawed lumber tickled my nose. Daddy had a door to the outside propped open and was rolling a refrigerator across some boards into the back of the truck.

"You about ready to go?" he asked.

"Soon as I get an iron for Miss McKenna that some people are buying."

The shelves in the back of Uncle Lesley's store were lined with odds and ends, and I found the iron between an alarm clock and a pair of shiny rubber work boots. The iron weighed about as much as a baby pig, and I studied its on-and-off button as I carried it back to the front of the store. Could heating an iron really be that easy?

"You look like you can't hardly bear to part with that," Miss McKenna said, smiling, taking it out of my hands.

I smelled her Evening in Paris perfume and thought of the midnight blue bottle that sat on Aunty Rose's dressing table.

A little later, Daddy and I drove through the countryside with its reddish soil. I helped watch for places where the highline was going in.

"Maybe that rancher there wants his place wired, Daddy," I said, pointing to a sprawling ranch of weathered buildings where no power lines marched up the lane from the road.

"Too many outbuildings," Daddy said, slowing down and studying it. "I need just a house for my first job. Maybe a house and a chicken house."

I'd seen Daddy, back home, poring over a book called *Farm Wiring for Light and Power, Prepared Especially for Home Study*.

Well, I hadn't started right off reading *Wuthering Heights* in first grade. I'd read about Dick and Jane back then. I watched the red hills roll by. That was what Daddy needed. A Dick-and-Jane wiring job.

That night, I sat on one side of the wobbly card table, writing to Aunty Rose on the Big Chief tablet we'd bought. Daddy sat across from me, working on Mrs. Stanton's alarm clock.

Mrs. Stanton, our landlady, lived right below us, and we could hear her radio playing.

"I hate living so close to people," I said to Daddy, laying my pencil down. "Hearing each little noise they make and smelling their food cooking."

He glanced up from settling the tiny gears back inside the clock, then bent back over his work.

"Don't you hate it, Daddy?" I insisted. Didn't he want to go home too?

"You should try living on a destroyer at sea for months at a time," he said, without looking up. "Now, that's being close to your fellow man."

The bright ceiling light threw my own shadow over the paper I was trying to write on. At home, I'd have just slid the lamp toward me.

I shut my eyes, letting the fan Uncle Lesley had given us blow across my face.

"I sure am glad you fixed this fan, Daddy."

He nodded, balancing a small screwdriver in the depths of the alarm clock gears.

I went back to reading what I had written in my first letter home.

August 23, 1947

Dear Aunty Rose,

We got here about dark yesterday. Our apartment is shabby with hardly any furniture. But guess what it does have! Electric lights and a bathroom. I took two baths yesterday and two already today. I may take another one tonight. You would love the bathtub, Aunty Rose.

I'm glad Nana sent all the food, but we still may starve to death. Daddy just knows navy cooking. Tonight he made rice and raisins. The raisins swelled up and looked like Jacky's ticks.

Also today Daddy bought electrician's supplies at Montgomery Ward, which took most of our money. But we did get a pancake turner, a pan, and some silverware. I hope soon we can get some dishes. Already I'm tired of eating out of quart jars and at The Pan.

Tomorrow we're having a sign painted on the truck.

. . . If I hadn't died of homesickness by then.

Why was being away from home in the evening worse than any other time of day?

I steadied my hand so my writing didn't shake as much as I was trembling inside.

> Remember your promise to write every day.
>> Love, Willa Mae
>
> P.S. Wish I could be there with you instead of on the other end of the earth. Maybe I'll just walk home.

Could I walk home? I stared into space, seeing myself beside the highway, a sack of peanut butter and jelly sandwiches in my hand, walking for days, dodging the army convoy trucks—walking back through the Ozarks and all those chenille bedspreads and across the bridge.

Mrs. Stanton's alarm clock going off on the card table snapped me out of my daydream.

Daddy beamed across the table at me. "Fixed it," he said, standing up. "Want to go with me to take it to Mrs. Stanton?"

"Sure thing," I said.

Chapter 10

The next day, Sunday, we drove to Onatanka to see a sign painter who owed Uncle Les a favor. We found the man, Mr. Kincaid, up in the hills behind a sweet potato farm.

We pulled the truck into an open-sided shed, then followed Mr. Kincaid's directions to a small green lake where Uncle Les swore there were fish so big, they'd bite off my toes if I didn't keep my shoes on.

I had never fished before, and the smell of the bait and the flapping of the fish in Daddy's hand as he worked the hooks free made my stomach roll. But I still kept throwing my line back in, hoping for a pull on it, because Daddy acted so proud when I caught one.

"They'll taste good for supper," he said, dropping a

bluegill in the bucket and stringing another worm on my hook.

As the day wore on, the sun beat down on us and a breeze whipped little waves against the sandy bank. When we had a bucket of catfish and bluegill, we made our way back to the sign painter's shed.

I wiped my fishy-smelling hands on the front of my clothes, thinking Nana would have a conniption if she saw the mud all over my dress and the rip from the barbed wire fence.

Mr. Kincaid, a wiry man with black hair that stuck up in spikes, leaned back with his elbows against his workbench as Daddy and I inspected the truck.

On the side, he'd painted a red circle with a yellow lightning bolt slashed through it. Then he had lettered

HAROLD CLARK, ELECTRICIAN
HOME, FARM, AND INDUSTRIAL WIRING

I looked at Daddy. Wouldn't *that* show those Green boys back home?

"How much I owe you?" Daddy asked, reaching for his billfold.

"Not a thing," Mr. Kincaid said, scratching at a dried

smear of yellow paint streaking his cheek. "Just tell Les Clark we're even."

Down the road, Daddy pulled in at the sweet potato farm and bought a half peck of sweet potatoes from an old man with a glass eye.

"You like these?" Daddy asked, setting the sack in the seat between us.

"I like them at Thanksgiving, the way Nana fixes them," I said, which made me wonder what Daddy and I would do at Thanksgiving, way out here in Oklahoma.

I rubbed my sunburned nose with my stinky-fish hands. I wanted to get cleaned up, then do girl things with Aunty Rose—paint our nails and look at patterns.

The truck growled as Daddy shifted into low for the switchback down out of the hills.

"You missing home?" he asked, glancing across the seat at me.

Daddy was getting pretty good at reading my mind.

I nodded.

"Me too," he said, his voice sounding like he'd been running.

"How can you be homesick, Daddy?" I stared out the window, the feathery trees that crowded the side of the road so close, I could reach out and touch them.

"I know I've been gone a long time," he said. "But in the service, even in wartime, they take care of you. A man doesn't have to worry about where his next meal's coming from. It may taste like old shoes, but it's coming from the mess three times a day regular as a ticking clock."

The words poured out of him. "A man doesn't have to worry about where he's going to sleep, or get his clothes, or anything except doing his job and staying alive. Now, when your mama lived. . . ."

His voice broke, and he stared at the horizon for a few seconds, then he went on, talking fast. "When she lived, I didn't have a second's doubt about anything. We were partners. We each took care of the other one. Now—"

When I glanced at Daddy, his face was all twisted up. I looked away, feeling it wasn't polite to stare. Daddy made a funny noise, back in his throat. He looked at me, his eyes sparkling with tears, but then he grinned.

"You know what, Mae Bug?" he said, hitting the brakes and pulling onto a track that ran down to the river. "I think I'm mainly hungry."

I hung on to the door handle as we bounced over gopher holes and head-high weeds scraped against the running boards.

Had Daddy gone crazy?

He rocked the truck to a stop on the flat stretch of gravel that ran along a slow, pretty little stream.

"We'll make us a bonfire and cook these fish and sweet potatoes. Might even catch crawdads for crawdaddy stew."

Daddy slid out of the truck and came around to my side, opening the door.

"Whatever we cook, it'll beat sitting in a furnished apartment with no furniture and eating cold stuff out of quart jars that makes us homesick just to look at it."

I felt all weak-kneed from the way Daddy was pouncing on the truth and laying it out in front of us. I guess that's why I started crying. I wrapped my arms around Daddy's waist, burying my face, feeling the racking of his body as he wept too.

When we were finally done, I listened to the quiet running of the river. Here we stood, hundreds of miles from home, with not much to our names but a truck with some fancy painting on it.

Daddy handed me his handkerchief. After I'd used it, I gave it back. His nose blowing scared a bird out of the bushes, which made us laugh as it went squawking off over the creek.

We walked along the bank, picking up driftwood.

Then we started a fire, and while it burned down to embers for cooking our potatoes, we pulled off our shoes and waded in the shallow, sandy-bottomed creek.

As the cool water swirled around our ankles, I considered telling Daddy about Grandpa's catching the water moccasin but decided not to. I asked about Mama instead. At home, she didn't seem so . . . *missing*. But with Daddy and me off by ourselves, I thought about her a lot more.

"Daddy, do you remember marrying Mama?" I asked.

Daddy's voice sounded funny when he said, "Sure, I do."

"Would you tell me about it?" I asked, without looking at him.

After a while, he said, "Well, we got married at the church. Your mama's friend, Marian, and my buddy from high school, Tom Luther, stood up with us. Old Bob Hewett performed the ceremony. At six o'clock in the evening."

We had stopped walking and stood with the water's current tangling our feet. I bent down for a bright blue pebble that winked in the water.

"What did Mama look like?" I asked, studying the stone, rubbing it with my thumb.

"Well, she looked a lot like you're starting to look," he said, putting his hand on my head. "She pushed her hair up real pretty, with flowers in it. She made me proud."

Daddy bent down and picked up a pebble too. "Your mama always felt close to her family," he said, his back to me. "So I kind of made them mine. Like I had two sets of folks."

I rubbed my arms in the sudden late-day chill.

Daddy smacked his neck. "Mosquitoes are hungry."

He looked at me then, and we smiled at each other.

"When you came along," he said, "I thought Will and Mae would pop with pride. I think they would have given me the world. Just because I was your daddy.

"But love's not always a good thing," Daddy said, reading my thoughts. "Your grandpa loved Treva so much, he went crazy when she died. Did you know he wouldn't let me see you when I came home?"

I caught my breath. "When did you come home?"

"After your mama died. As soon as they could get me off the ship. I was on a shakedown cruise up the coast. You didn't know that?"

I shook my head.

"I rode the train for three days, about dead with grief. Feeling so sorry for you. And Mae and Will. But when I got home, Will wouldn't see me. Wouldn't let me see you.

151

And about that time, the Japs attacked Pearl Harbor, and all leaves were canceled. So I had to just get back on that ship and take my feelings out on the enemy. I couldn't hardly raise a little girl on a destroyer in the middle of the ocean," Daddy said. "And I knew you'd get plenty of love with Will and Mae."

He was sure right about that.

"Why'd you come back now, Daddy?"

"Because the war's over, Mae Bug."

I made a sound, half laugh, half cry. The war wasn't over. It was still going on right inside me. Grandpa in the north, Daddy in the south.

"I mean, why'd you come back for me?"

"Because it seemed right."

I waited for more. That didn't sound like much of a reason for turning a person's world upside down.

"That's the only way I know to explain it, Mae Bug."

He stood there in the rippling water, his pants rolled up to his knees, looking at me with a plea for understanding in his eyes.

Maybe it *did* seem right. But it didn't seem *enough*. I needed Nana and Grandpa and Aunty Rose too.

"And what about the baby?" I asked. "Why is he set apart like he doesn't belong?"

Fierceness crossed Daddy's face. "I swear I don't know. I guess your grandpa just went crazy." His voice whipped with anger. "But he sure shamed me. For two cents I'd just dig up that little casket and move it right over by your mama where it belongs."

I cringed at the thought of the storm that would rip our family apart for good if Daddy did any such thing.

I heard him breathing and he said finally, in a calmer voice, "I guess we better clean those fish and get them in the fire."

After our meal, as we lay on a flat rock and watched young hawks ride the updraft, I half shut my eyes and nearly fell asleep, finding it easier to sleep out in the open, with the water babbling around me, than penned up in the apartment.

"Sing about that gypsy, Daddy," I said, staring at the first star in the twilight. I hated the idea of the blue-eyed baby being left behind, but I was starting to like the gypsy Davy and his big guitar.

Chapter 11

Early the next morning, with the hills purple in the gentle light, Daddy and I found our first house to wire.

Mr. and Mrs. Mullins, the old couple who lived in the little asphalt-shingled house where the dam road met Highway 56, kept chickens and had a big garden with hollyhocks that made me think of home.

"Leon and I want to die among a few modern conveniences," Mrs. Mullins said, tucking threads of silver hair into her bun.

The whiff of pancakes and bacon still hung around the screen door, and Mrs. Mullins handed me a big crockery cup warm with sweet, milky coffee. I sat down on the porch to drink it, trying to hear what the men were saying over by the truck.

Daddy had his back to me. "Take about thirty working hours," he said to Mr. Mullins, sounding like we'd been in the wiring business since 1937 right along with the Green boys. But I saw Daddy squeezing the fingers of his left hand together as if he were pumping himself up.

Stroking the spine of the calico cat that came to rub against my legs, I held my breath.

"And I'll need fifty dollars for the job," Daddy said.

Would somebody really pay us that much money?

I could tell by the stiffness of Daddy's back that he was holding his breath too.

Finally Mr. Mullins stuck out his hand to cinch the deal, and I exhaled slowly.

When Daddy looked at me, his face glowed like somebody had lit a Christmas candle inside him. He turned our truck around and parked it so anybody passing could read the sign on the side.

I helped him lug the blowtorch, the toolbox, and wiring materials onto the porch.

"You going to work with your daddy every day, honey?" Mrs. Mullins asked. "Do we have to pay extra for you?"

"No, ma'am," I said. "I'm part of the deal."

"She's my apprentice," Daddy said, glancing at me. The way he said it made it clear I was a real helper and not just a tagalong. "She's a pretty good mechanic too."

Mrs. Mullins leaned her head to one side, looking at me, and I felt embarrassed. Maybe Mrs. Mullins agreed with Nana that fixing cars and wiring houses weren't fit pastimes for a girl.

I held the door open while Daddy carried inside two rolls of Romex electrical cable, one on each shoulder.

In no time, he was giving me a hand over the top of the ladder into the Mullinses' hot attic.

"Stay on the cross beams," he cautioned me. "Mrs. Mullins won't want our feet sticking through the ceiling."

I felt like a tightrope walker, brushing away the cobwebs, then squatting down to steady the kerosene lantern for Daddy.

His face already beaded with sweat, he began to poke and snake a little metal cable between the wall that divided the kitchen from the living room.

I saw a dead bird lodged in one of the cross beams. It had been dead a long time and had dried out, showing a lacework of skeletal bones and mysterious openings.

Quick as an eye blink, a spider the size of my palm darted under a cross beam.

Sheets of sweat formed on the backs of my legs.

A pearl of moisture slid the length of Daddy's nose and dripped onto his dungarees. "I got out twelve feet of snake," he said.

"What's that mean?"

"Means we can get through with cable here. Mrs. Mullins wants an outlet on this wall." He reeled in the snake and clipped it on his tool belt.

Back down in the living room, we cut an opening for Mrs. Mullins's outlet and Daddy began to push the snake up through the hole.

"You willing to go back up in the attic by yourself?" he asked quietly, so Mrs. Mullins wouldn't hear in the kitchen.

I nodded, trying to forget the spider.

Daddy squeezed my arm. "When you see the tip of the snake, coil the end of the Romex around it," he said. "Sing out when you're done."

"Okay," I said.

He held the ladder steady until I stepped off it and onto the cross beams.

What Daddy had told me to do wasn't easy, because

the thick Romex was hard to twist. My first two coils slipped loose, but I kept starting over and finally yelled down, "Ready!"

"Good," he yelled back. "Now I'm going to pull on the snake. You just ease the Romex off the roll and make sure it follows along."

"Okay," I called.

And so the morning went, with Daddy putting outlets and switches and overhead lights where Mrs. Mullins wanted them.

In the afternoon, I held the soldering cup while he dipped the bare wires in solder and twisted them together.

"The REA inspector will examine these junctions real close," he said. "If they're not just right, I'll have to do them over."

At the end of the day, we drove back to the apartment, worn out. I stared at the palms of my hands, black from the Romex. Daddy looked fierce, with black lines smearing his face and clots of cobwebs matting his hair.

Mrs. Stanton had slid our mail under the door to our apartment, and I almost stepped on the letter from home. I ripped it open, then held the pages over my heart, as if that would connect me with home even for a second.

Daddy caught me doing that, and he looked away.

Reading as I walked through the apartment, I climbed out the little half door at the end of the hall that led right up to the roof.

Oklahoma was a funny place, where people got out and walked on their flat roofs. Daddy had strung up a clothesline so we could dry our wet clothes after we washed them in the bathtub. I sat on an upside-down bucket someone had left.

Nana had sent two pictures from our album at home. There was Aunty Rose and me, kneeling in the grass on the west side of the house. We had our arms around Jacky, who grinned at the camera, his tongue lolling out. Grandpa had taken the picture, and his long shadow fell on the grass and up the side of the house, bigger than life. I ached to stand close to him and smell his Lifebuoy soap.

In the picture of Nana and Grandpa on the side porch, their eyes seemed to be looking right into mine.

Nana wrote:

I sent the pictures so you don't forget us. Rose and I canned twenty-four quarts of tomatoes today. Tomorrow I'm going to make juice out of what's left. I hope your daddy is feeding you good.

If I'd had any idea you'd be leaving us, I'd have

taught you how to cook. I guess I just thought you were ours to keep.

The rest of the words blurred as I wiped away the tears. I was wiping my nose on the back of my hand when Daddy came up through the trapdoor.

I put the letter back in the envelope and turned away. I felt Daddy standing there and wished he'd leave.

"I reckon you pretty well hate me for taking you away," he said.

His throat sounded as tight as mine felt.

I didn't answer.

"Your granddad hurt me too," he said. "I loved Will and Mae like they were my own folks."

I swallowed. What did he expect me to say?

"When your mama died, seems like I lost about half the people I loved. You. Your grandparents. Rose."

I nodded, not looking at him, wondering if my throat might explode with pain.

"And I had to fight a war on top of everything else," he said. "I just couldn't hardly stand it, some days."

"But I can't hardly stand it now," I said, turning around and letting him see the tears running down my face.

I waited, hoping he might pet me and say we could go

160

home soon, but he didn't. And I couldn't see the look on his face because I was crying so much.

After a while, he turned around and left the rooftop. But I stayed up there a long time, finally finishing the letters and looking at the pictures again and again.

Aunty Rose wrote:

Dear Willa Mae,

I keep watching for you, just expecting to see you walk in my room or come across the road from the pasture with Dad. Mom had one of her sick headaches today. She misses you like anything and worries. Dad's acting like a cow without its calf. It was surely mean of your daddy to take you away. I never thought he would do such a thing. If you write every day, like we promised each other, I should get a letter from you Saturday or Monday. I'm going to Walnut Hill with Charles Michael tonight. I wish you were here to help me paint my nails. I finished the red dress and hope it looks pretty on the dance floor. Let me know how your daddy is treating you.

Hugs and kisses, R.

"I'm out of the bathroom." Daddy stuck his head through the opening to the roof.

He looked scrubbed and hopeful and tired, but I could tell by the way he stopped half in and half out of the little door that he wondered if I was still mad at him for dragging me off to Oklahoma.

"You about ready to eat?" he asked.

I stood up, putting the letters and pictures back in the envelope.

"Let me get a bath first."

Daddy took my hand to help me through the door to the roof as if I hadn't gone through it a dozen times by myself.

In the bathtub, I soaked and scrubbed, watching clean skin appear under the grime.

Daddy dried my hair while we sat up on the roof. Then, as darkness fell, we spooned out what we wanted from a quart of Nana's peaches and a quart of her blackberries.

"Should I fry some Spam?" Daddy asked me when we were done.

I shook my head. The cool, sweet juiciness of the fruit had satisfied me.

I collapsed on my pallet that night, holding Daddy's hand, my last thought being that as much as I had missed everyone, I had forgotten to write home.

Chapter 12

We'd been in Oklahoma a week by the time we finished wiring the Mullinses' house and Daddy's work passed inspection.

The Friday afternoon the REA man came out to the Mullinses' place, wearing a safety helmet with the REA logo on it, I almost forgot to breathe as he went from junction to junction and connection to connection. He tugged cables and peered into holes.

When I glanced at Daddy, his face looked as confident as Abe Lincoln on the side of a penny, but he was opening and closing the fingers on his left hand.

Finally the inspector nodded to Daddy. "Screw 'em down," he said, gesturing at the switch plates and outlets

Daddy had had to leave hanging loose until they passed inspection.

Daddy pulled a screwdriver off his tool belt and got to work, and I stood right beside him, ready to help if he needed me.

As soon as the inspector installed the meter on the pole, he turned on the electricity and the Mullinses' house lit up. The day was overcast, and when the fixture came on over the kitchen table, Mrs. Mullins clapped and said, "It's just like the sun's come out."

We packed up the last of the tools, then pulled onto the highway with Mr. Mullins's fifty dollars in Daddy's pocket. Daddy radiated happiness like the pictures of the apostles with gold around their heads in the Bible.

"You bring light to the world, Daddy," I teased him on the way back to town.

The next two weeks brought Daddy a steady flow of business. Mr. Mullins had a nephew who needed his place wired. And Mr. Mullins's nephew knew a rancher with a bunch of outbuildings who was looking for a wiring expert to handle his spread. And Uncle Les had a friend the next county over who needed work done.

Daddy would listen while people told him what they wanted, then nod and say, "I can do that."

We worked every day—even on Sunday unless the people he was wiring for had something against it. I was careful not to mention that in the letters home. And every day I went with him, climbing around in attics and haylofts and chicken houses, helping him snake cable. We'd only been away from home for three weeks, but my hands seemed permanently lined with black.

I liked being his helper, and after a while, I didn't even need to be told what to do. Daddy would just meet my eyes and nod when I figured it out for myself. When we'd get in the truck at the end of the day, both so tired and filthy we could hardly move, he'd put his hand on my head and let it rest there for a minute. Then we'd drive fast through the hills, making the air blow through the cab of the truck to cool us off.

Our money started to stack up. Fifty dollars. A hundred dollars. Two hundred dollars. Four hundred dollars. Although Daddy had customers signed up waiting for him to come wire their houses, one night when we were eating Spam and eggs up on the roof, Daddy announced we were going to take the next day, Tuesday, off.

"Why?" I said.

I didn't miss home so much when we were busy working. In fact, sometimes when we were pushing to get a job done in three days so we could get on to the next one, I'd forget my homesickness altogether. I stopped thinking, *Well, this is Saturday, so Nana and Aunty Rose will be cleaning. This is Sunday, so they'll all be going to church. This is Monday, so they'll be doing the wash.*

So why did Daddy want to take a day off? Idleness was the devil's playground, as Grandpa said.

"Well," Daddy answered me, "we can't keep living like gypsies." He wiggled his eyebrows, trying to make me laugh. "Before long it will get too cold to sit up on this roof and eat supper. We'll have icicles hanging from our ears."

"But it's nice up here," I said, looking at the purple sky splashed with stars like the inside of a magician's cape.

"We need a bed for you to sleep in," Daddy went on. "And an iron, so we can tend to our clothes. And some real dishes."

"No," I said, my fierceness making Daddy blink.

If I had a bed, somehow that would root us in this place. And I didn't want roots here. I didn't want Oklahoma dishes.

"But Mae Bug," Daddy said. "We're living all ragtag. What would your grandmother say?"

166

I set down my plate, not wanting any more of my supper though I'd felt half starved when I'd smelled the Spam frying. "I need things . . ."

Daddy waited while I tried to figure out how to explain it to him.

"I need things that aren't here."

Daddy set his plate down too and stood looking at the stars, not saying anything.

In her last letter, Aunty Rose had written:

I get so lonesome for you, Shorty, and so do Mom and Dad. I think Dad could even be nice to Harold now. For your sake. He lost your mama. He doesn't want to lose you too.

Why couldn't I get Daddy to try again?

"We could go home now," I said. "We've got some money, and you've got some confidence in your house wiring. We've got a fine truck. You could give those Green boys a run for their money."

"You still want to go that bad?" Daddy finally asked, his voice sounding tired in the darkness.

"Yes, sir," I said. "More than anything."

We took the next day off, but didn't go shopping for furniture. We went fishing. The leaves were starting to turn yellow, and we saw pumpkins fattening in the fields as we drove up to the little green lake behind the sweet potato farm.

School would be starting soon, and I found myself remembering the sights and smells of the first day, everybody so starched and polished they practically cracked when they sat in their seats. The windows shining from the teacher's elbow grease and vinegar water. The flag at the top of the pole, against the sun, snapping and ruffling as we pledged our allegiance.

I guess Daddy was thinking too, because he was quiet. His eyes looked sleepy, and once when I was taking a fish off my hook and dropping it in the bucket, I noticed he'd leaned back in the grass and fallen asleep. I watched little tadpoles playing around the murky edges until he woke up, then we ate the peanut butter and jelly sandwiches we'd brought along.

While we were eating, a train passed through the valley just out of sight over the hills.

"Trains make a lonesome sound," Daddy said.

I nodded and tossed a crust in the water, watching to see if a big fish rose for it.

"After the attack on Pearl Harbor, all the servicemen on leave were scrambling to get back to their posts," Daddy said. "Dad took me to the train station in Huxley and saw me get on the train."

I stared at the still, green water and listened to the whistle of the train in the quiet valley. I tried to imagine the world suddenly at war, servicemen racing to get on ships and airplanes to fight for our country.

"As soon as Dad shook my hand and turned away, I walked on through the train car and down the steps on the other side. I couldn't bring myself to stay on that train. I didn't care that the Japanese had blown up Pearl Harbor. My life had been blown up a lot worse. Your mama was dead. I wasn't allowed even a glimpse of you, which was what I needed more than anything."

Daddy closed his fingers around my arm, and I nodded.

"My second family had turned their backs on me. Will had lost his senses. The baby was all by himself in the cemetery."

I knew for sure now that Daddy had loved Mama. And he loved me. He must have been mighty hurt by the way Grandpa acted.

"So I just let that train pull out without me," he said.

"Did you catch the next train, Daddy? And still get back on time?"

Daddy shook his head, staring at his red-and-white bobber floating in the water. "I laid low in Huxley for days, trying to talk some sense into myself."

"You didn't go AWOL, did you?"

He nodded, not meeting my eyes.

I'd seen enough war movies to know that people who were absent without leave were cowardly people who didn't have the gumption to fight for our country. Grandpa had been in the infantry in World War I and gone clear to France on a cattle boat. And he hadn't been afraid. He wasn't even afraid to catch a water moccasin to show me the cotton mouth.

"So did you get in trouble?" I asked.

Daddy shook his head. "I finally accepted the fact that I had to do my duty, even if I didn't want to. Even if I didn't feel in any kind of shape to be running the communications on a destroyer. I went back. I was three days late, and my commanding officer could have let me get in a lot of hot water. But he knew how it was."

Daddy studied my face, trying to read my thoughts.

"He was a good man. He just fixed up the records some way and got me back on the ship."

I didn't want Daddy reading my thoughts, so I turned away, pretending to untangle a worm from the coffee can full of bait. I put it on the hook and threw the line out, the bobber making a big splash in the silence.

"How'd we get on this subject, anyway?" Daddy said after a while. "I've not told that story to anybody before."

"The train," I said, watching the water tremble around the bobber. "The train down in the valley made you think of it."

"Yeah," he said. "That and your wanting to go home so much." After a pause, he added, "I guess I know how you feel."

❧   ❧   ❧

In the next few days, we finished up the last two jobs that Daddy had committed to. He never did say for sure that we'd be going home when we were done. But he didn't say any more about buying furniture and dishes, and he didn't take on any more jobs.

I wrote Aunty Rose:

I don't want to get your hopes up, but maybe Daddy is thinking of coming back. He's done real good at finding jobs in Oklahoma, and he could have a lot more. But he knows how much I miss you all. I just want to come home and see everybody. See how much my lamb has grown. I want to talk to you and go back to the way things were.

I looked over what I had written. Every word was true. But there was more that maybe Aunty Rose wouldn't be able to understand. I liked helping Daddy wire houses. I liked holding his hand at night until one of us went to sleep. I liked the magical music that poured out of him sometimes. I liked the way he dried my hair, as if it was the most important job in the world. I liked the way he tried to take care of me, even if it was jelly sandwiches and navy cooking.

Chapter 13

Daddy never did say for sure that we'd be going home until we were packing up the tools after finishing our last job on Wednesday afternoon, so I didn't get a chance to write with the news. But it was just as well, or they would have worn themselves out watching for us.

Daddy and I traveled home the same way we came, except the truck was loaded with tools and equipment instead of Nana's canned goods, plus Daddy had almost five hundred dollars in his pocket.

We packed peanut butter and jelly sandwiches and filled some of Nana's empty mason jars with drinking water. As we drove through the Ozarks, I wished I had money to buy Nana a pretty chenille bedspread.

"Which bedspread do you like better, Daddy?" I asked, pointing to a clothesline in front of a weathered house in the side of the hill. "Peacocks or butterflies?"

Daddy looked at the display ruffling in the wind. "Either one is nice," he said.

Daddy didn't seem to understand that you were supposed to pick one.

"Well, which one would Mama have liked best?"

"She'd have liked the butterfly one," he said. "She always thought butterflies were real pretty."

When Daddy told me things Mama liked and did, and how she looked, she seemed to come alive again inside me. At first, the stirring memories would hurt, but the more I touched them, the nicer it felt.

After the interesting things for sale disappeared in the rearview mirror, I read Daddy some stories from my book.

When my voice got hoarse, I opened a jar of water and offered Daddy a drink, then took one myself.

"How much farther to the Mississippi River?" I asked.

"Just a little ways."

But it seemed to take forever.

Finally a silver twist of water glinted between the hills, and I watched the river grow bigger and broader as we dropped into the valley and wended our way to the bridge that spanned the water.

On the bridge, I hung out the window. A long barge train loaded with golden grain passed beneath us.

"We're back in our home state, Daddy," I told him as we drove off the bridge on the other side.

"Yep. We've only been gone a month," he said. "Things don't look much different."

We ate the rest of the peanut butter and jelly sandwiches and drank all the water, not because we were hungry or thirsty, but because we didn't know what else to do.

Daddy tried singing to pass the time, but right then I just wanted him to be still and concentrate on getting us home as fast as he could.

In a while he stopped singing and shifted in his seat, squaring his shoulders. He came up on a truck carrying chicken crates, tooted, and went around. Then he gave our truck more gas and passed everything that turned up in front of us all the way to Huxley.

A few hours later, we stopped at a filling station just west of town. A man who worked there read the sign on the door and asked Daddy if he wanted any more customers. Daddy said sure and got directions to where the man lived.

"He didn't say a word about the Green boys," I said as we drove away.

"Maybe they've left the country."

"If they've not, maybe you could run them out," I suggested.

"There's probably enough work to go around," Daddy said and smiled. It was nice that he'd landed a job close to home.

"What do you suppose everybody will be doing when we get there?" I asked.

"Well, I reckon your grandma will be doing something in the kitchen. Maybe finishing up the supper dishes."

"And Aunty Rose will be writing me a letter," I said. "That's what she does every night after supper."

Where would Grandpa be? I thought.

When we turned in the drive, the special purple light that comes right before starry darkness wrapped the house and barn and other buildings. Pale lamplight glowed through the kitchen and sunroom windows.

"You know what, Daddy?" I said. "It sure is dark in the country."

"Sure is," he agreed. "And I like that. Maybe all this electricity isn't such a good idea."

Daddy's voice had a cheerfulness to it that suddenly sounded forced. Was he dreading meeting Grandpa again?

As I slid out of the truck, Jacky came charging out of the shadows and bumped against my thigh, nearly knocking me over as he wagged his whole body. He groaned and whined as I patted him and squatted down to hug his head.

"We got company?" I heard Nana say from the back door. "Who's out there?"

"Nana! It's me."

I heard her coming down the steps as I ran toward her. Burying myself in her body and feeling her arms close around me, I shut my eyes. My stomach, my heart, and even my fingers and toes warmed. Something hummed inside me that said the whole world might whirl in noise and darkness, but I was safe at the center.

"Who's out there?" Grandpa called from the doorway.

"It's me," I said, pulling away from Nana and running to him. "And my daddy. We've come home." Grandpa picked me up in his arms and swung me around like I was a little girl.

"Well, sure enough!" he said.

I felt the collar of his denim shirt and the straps of his overalls under my hands.

"Willa Mae? Willa Mae?" Aunty Rose ran out the door, shrieking, and let the screen bang behind her.

Grandpa set me down and Aunty Rose hugged me until I couldn't breathe and had to push her away.

I heard the truck door slam as Daddy got out.

"Daddy did real good in Oklahoma," I said, standing back away from everybody and making an announcement. "He made almost five hundred dollars wiring houses. Now he's brought me home so I can start school."

Daddy and I had never talked about school starting, but it sounded like as good a reason as any to explain his kindness.

"Well, that's just fine," Nana said, her voice practically singing in the darkness.

"School hasn't started already, has it?" I didn't want to miss the first day.

"Starts Monday," Grandpa said. "I went down and mowed the school yard today."

Silence fell among us. I could feel Nana and Grandpa wanting to get me inside. And Aunty Rose gripped my hand, pulling me toward the door as she danced around.

"Well," Daddy said, "I know Willa Mae will want to stay here tonight. And I need to see the folks."

I heard the truck door slam, and I slipped free of Aunty Rose to run and stand by Daddy's window.

I peered through the open truck window at Daddy's face, pale in the darkness. He seemed small compared to Grandpa. In Oklahoma, he had seemed bigger.

"Grandmother and Grandfather Clark will sure be glad to see you," I said. "And Aunt Belle."

He nodded.

"Will you tell them I said hello?" I asked. "And I'll see them soon. Thank you for bringing me home, Daddy."

"You're welcome," he said, putting the truck into reverse. "Sleep tight. Don't let the bedbugs bite."

I laughed. A bedbug wouldn't last two seconds in Nana's house, and Daddy knew it.

"See you later," I said, leaping onto the running board and putting my hand on his head, as he had done to mine a million times.

Inside, everything was just as I'd left it. The kitchen still smelled of wood from the cookstove. I could taste the grime of our trip on my lips and longed for a good bath. The memory of the big, white bathtub in Oklahoma loomed in my mind.

The floor in the doorway between the kitchen and dining room still squeaked when I passed through. A lamp burned in the middle of the dining-room table, and Aunty Rose's stationery was spread out just as I'd thought it would be. I grabbed up the robin salt and pepper shakers off the table.

"I just love these old salt and pepper shakers," I announced, giving each one of them a big smack.

Everybody was staring at me like I'd gone crazy. Then we started laughing. I hung on to Aunty Rose and laughed until tears poured down my face.

Nana warmed up some fried potatoes and lima beans for me and she fried bacon. Everybody watched me eat, and the food tasted so good.

My own bed was a welcome place, and I fell asleep wondering what Daddy was doing.

First thing Saturday morning I went across the pasture with Grandpa and checked on my livestock. The woods to the east glowed with patches of gold leaves, and Jacky went dashing into the undergrowth, on the scent of some animal.

My lamb had filled out in the time I'd been gone and nearly knocked me over trying to get to the bucket of mash Grandpa carried.

"Seems like everything is back in its right place now. Reckon your daddy will stay around here?" Grandpa asked on the way back to the house for breakfast.

"I hope so," I said.

"Reckon he'll leave you with us?"

I looked up at Grandpa, longing to find an expression in his eyes that wouldn't make me choose to live with one or the other.

"I don't know," I said.

Even from the road, I could smell Nana's biscuits, and I ran on ahead, anxious to find Aunty Rose and tell her about sitting on the roof for our meals in Oklahoma.

❧   ❧   ❧

Daddy didn't come around until the next afternoon. We were just finishing up Sunday dinner when I heard the truck. I asked to be excused and ran out to greet him.

"How are you?" he asked.

"Fine."

Daddy looked as if he'd been enjoying some of Grandmother Clark's good food the last couple of days. And his eyes shone.

"Come in, Harold," Nana called, stepping out the door. "We're just about to have some pie."

I knew Nana must have asked Grandpa if Daddy could come in and sit down at the table with us, and my heart warmed that Grandpa had said yes.

"Thanks, Mae," Daddy said. "That sounds real good."

He got out of the truck, then reached across the seat for a box.

"What's that?" I asked, bouncing to see.

The box was gray-and-white striped, and the words *The Mammoth Department Store* were lettered in red.

"Something for you," Daddy said.

The Mammoth was a store in Huxley that I'd walked by a hundred times, but Nana said everything in there would be too high for us.

"I bought you something special to wear the first day of school," Daddy said, watching my face. "Open it," he went on, his voice shaking. "Here. I'll hold the bottom. You pull off the lid."

The sound of the lid sliding off and sucking up tissue paper gave me goosebumps.

"Daddy!"

I lifted out the jade-colored dress with a little pink butterfly pattern all through the material and a collar made out of a soft white fabric.

"It's beautiful," I said, then wheeled to run into the house, leaving Daddy to bring the box and tissue paper.

"Look!"

I screeched to a stop in the dining room with the dress up against me.

"It'll fit perfectly and it came from The Mammoth and Daddy bought it for the first day of school."

I twirled around, holding the dress to my waist, then stopped with one arm stuck out like a model in the Sears, Roebuck catalog.

After a while I quit drinking in the beauty of the dress, the pucker of smocking across the front, the tiny pleats at the waistline, and glanced up at the expressions on everybody's faces.

Aunty Rose's eyes gleamed with admiration.

Nana seemed caught up in calculating how she might have made that dress herself. She reached out a hand and rubbed the green paisley between her fingers and stroked the soft collar.

"That's fine material," she said.

I wasn't sure about Grandpa's expression. He didn't know much about girls' dresses, but I saw respect in his eyes.

The next morning, I took a picture postcard of the Mississippi River to school to show everybody. And as we stood around the flagpole I pledged allegiance to the flag with the other students, Marilee on one side of me and Mattie on the other.

I'd never looked finer for a first day. I loved the deep jade color of my dress. I loved the soft feel of the collar at my throat. Most of all I loved how Daddy had picked it out and bought it for me, and that it had butterflies Mama would have liked.

Chapter 14

One Saturday afternoon in late September, when Nana and Grandpa went down to Lorrimer's to do the trading, I stayed home to help Aunty Rose finish hemming a dress to wear that night.

We worked in the sunroom, me sitting cross-legged on the floor, a yardstick in my right hand and the strawberry-shaped pincushion on my knee, and Aunty Rose standing in front of me.

"I wish I had a daddy to get me store-bought dresses," Aunty Rose said, lifting her hair off her neck. "It would be a whole lot easier."

"Put your arms down," I said. "It hikes up the hem."

Aunty Rose dropped her arms and I measured up fourteen inches from the floor and slipped in a straight pin.

"Turn," I said.

Aunty Rose moved slightly and I measured and pinned again.

Through the open sunroom windows, I could hear wind moving through the trees, and the leaves made a dry sound. The sky glowed with the clear blue stillness of September.

The grandfather clock at the foot of the stairs struck twice.

I'd fallen back into my familiar, easy rhythms, but it was a little like walking with a rock in my favorite shoe.

"Are you ever going to tell me what makes the bad blood between Daddy and Grandpa?" I asked, tugging on Aunty Rose's hem to say she should turn again.

When she didn't answer, I looked up from my pinning, but she didn't meet my eyes.

"I hate living this way," I said, sliding in another pin. "It's like having my life split right down the middle."

Aunty Rose ignored me. "Do you suppose your daddy will buy you more dresses?" she asked.

"Well, he's not hardly going to make them for me. He can fix stuff, but he can't sew that I know of."

"You know what I mean," Aunty Rose said, turning a little. "Mom and I can keep making you clothes. And you're getting pretty good yourself."

I could sew simple things like plain skirts with elastic waistbands, but I could never make a collar or put in a zipper.

"But that's not the point." I steered Aunty Rose back to the subject. "I'm old enough to know why Daddy and Grandpa don't like each other. I've been clear to Oklahoma and back. Crossed the biggest river in the United States. Twice," I said, pinning again. "And if you don't tell me, I'm going to ask Grandpa."

"You wouldn't dare," Aunty Rose said.

"Well, I know it has something to do with my little brother," I told her, looking to see how she'd take the news that I knew about Baby Clark.

Aunty Rose's mouth dropped so wide, I could almost see China.

I kept measuring and pinning, letting her get used to the idea.

"How did you find out?" she finally asked.

"Daddy told me way back in the summer. One night when we were down at the cemetery."

"What did he tell you, exactly?"

"He said he didn't have any idea why Grandpa buried the baby over by himself, but that it shamed Mama. Shamed us all."

Then for good measure, I added, "Daddy said I should ask Grandpa why." I let that rest for a beat. "So that's what I'm going to do."

In the silence, I could hear the hens cackling over at the henhouse and somebody's tractor running in the distance.

"If I show you something, will you promise never, ever to tell?" Aunty Rose said.

My fingers stopped in the middle of pushing a pin through the fabric.

"Yes!"

"Then hurry and finish pinning," she said. "We have to do it before Mom and Dad get home."

"Do what?" I said, going as fast as I could, my hands shaking.

"You'll see," Aunty Rose replied.

When I scooted back and said, "Done," Aunty Rose slid off the new dress and pulled on her everyday skirt and sweater.

"We've got to hurry," she said, struggling with the button on her skirt.

"Hurry and what?" I flexed my hands, my palms damp with sweat.

"You'll see," she said again.

I don't know what I thought Aunty Rose was going to show me, but I was surprised when she led me into Nana and Grandpa's bedroom.

The window was up a crack to let in the breeze. The afternoon sun fell across Nana's folded yellow quilt lying on the cedar chest.

The house made settling noises in the silence, and we looked at each other, knowing it was wrong to snoop in other people's possessions. My ears strained for the sound of the car in the driveway.

Aunty Rose squatted in front of Grandpa's side of the double-sided oak bureau and opened the bottom drawer.

My face prickled as Grandpa's papers and other private things lay naked before us.

I sat down on the floor beside Aunty Rose as she fingered through gray business envelopes tied together with string, a packet of letters, a small brown box on which somebody had penciled *Accounts, 1940–1945*. She moved aside a worn leather spectacle case, a pair of binoculars, and the box Grandpa's watch from Montgomery Ward had come in. I saw a fat manila envelope with the cards and pictures I'd made for Grandpa over the years sticking out one end.

From near the bottom of the drawer, Aunty Rose picked up a small square of folded paper and held it out to me.

"What is it?" I said, moving my hands back.

"A letter from your daddy."

It was the tiniest letter I'd ever seen, about three by three, written on strange, slick paper.

"Why is it so small?" I said, feeling it between my thumb and finger.

"They did that during the war. It's called V mail. They shrunk up the servicemen's letters to save on cargo space."

I stared at the sheet of paper as she unfolded it.

"It's from your daddy to your mama," Aunty Rose said. "The last letter she got from him. You don't have to read every bit of it. The part that caused all the trouble is right here."

Aunty Rose had had a lot of experience with this letter. I took it from her and read the part where she pointed, straining to make out the tiny words:

. . . got a letter from Kyle Rogers today. He told me some things that made me real mad. He told me you'd

been stepping out on me and that maybe the baby isn't mine. Now, I don't believe him, and reckon he did it just to get even over that deal with the car last summer, but his letter still got me thinking. I don't want it to come between us, so I want you just to answer me yes or no. Have you done me wrong? And if the answer is no, I'll never give another thought to it, I promise you that.

Aunty Rose was watching my face.

"Do you know what your daddy is talking about?" she asked, her own face red.

I nodded. I felt dirty prying into Grandpa's things and reading words not intended for me, but my heart was racing to understand the mystery that had torn my family apart.

"I guess I always knew it had something to do with the baby," I whispered, my mouth dry.

"Well, when Treva got that letter, she went storming outside," Aunty Rose said. "Sleet was falling, and that's when the accident happened. And I guess she was going . . ." Aunty Rose made a question with her hands. "I don't know where she was going. Maybe just to show the letter to Mom, who was over at the henhouse, gathering eggs. But Treva's feet must have hit the icy steps and shot out from under her. I heard her fall. When I got there, she was unconscious. . . ."

My last memory of Mama bobbed to the surface for the first time in years. I saw her wind-chilled rosy face as she helped me into the car. She'd driven me down to the Clarks' that November morning to make cookies with Grandmother Clark and Aunt Belle. The wind had been biting, and we'd bundled up and worn our matching rabbit-skin muffs to keep our hands warm. Mama's hands had been startlingly warm against my cold cheeks when she kissed me good-bye.

Aunty Rose's face came back into focus. "—screamed and screamed," she was saying. "And I thought neither Mom nor Dad would ever come. But finally Dad came running from across the road, where he'd been watering the sheep. And he picked your mama up and carried her inside. I knew Dad would make it all right. He'd bring Treva back."

I nodded. "I know," I whispered, my tongue barely able to form the words. "I thought I could bring her back too." Tears rolled down my cheeks and dripped on my arm as I gripped the tiny letter. "I never told anybody, but I knew if I wished hard enough, she would come back to me."

Aunty Rose took a deep breath and I shrugged, not able to tell her how crushed I'd been when my wishing power hadn't been strong enough.

After a while, I cleared my throat and wiped my eyes with my shirttail.

"Tell me the rest," I urged, my voice hoarse.

"Well, Mom and I stayed with Treva, and Dad went tearing down to Uncle Retus's for some of them to go get Doc Simmons. The doctor didn't turn up here until almost seven. Treva was still unconscious, all that time lying on the couch in the sunroom where Dad had put her down. Dad sat beside her, in a chair, staring at her, his face like stone. I was crying because I didn't want Treva to die, and Mom kept rubbing her hands."

I wiped tears off the letter, then I folded it and handed it back to Aunty Rose.

"When the doctor got here, he said Treva had to go to the hospital in Huxley, so Uncle Retus went to Leghorn's funeral home in Mills and had them bring the hearse, and that's what they took your mama to the hospital in. Mom and Dad and I followed in the car. Dad told Uncle Retus to go down to the Clarks' and tell them Treva was in a bad way, but to keep the news from you."

I remembered not having anything to sleep in that night and asking why Mama hadn't come back for me. Grandmother Clark had stilled my worries with stories of sledding on the hill in the morning if the sleet turned to snow, and I'd gone to bed wearing one of Aunt Belle's slips. In the night, I'd woken up, feeling something was being taken out of my body. It was as if God had reached into my middle and lifted out something I'd never even realized was there. The next morning, I'd wanted to tell Grandmother Clark about the feeling, but I didn't know how to explain it.

"So was my little brother born then?" I asked. "Did he die that night?"

Aunty Rose drew in her breath. She nodded.

"Why didn't I know about the baby?" I asked.

"Well, you were practically a baby yourself," Aunty Rose said. "You'd have found out soon enough if everything had gone the way it was supposed to."

Aunty Rose slumped, her face in her hands, worn out from the story.

The little piece of V mail lay on the floor between us. I stared at it—the accidental trigger to Mama's and the baby's deaths. But why couldn't it have gone up in flames or blown away in the winter wind before Grandpa saw it?

"When did Grandpa find the letter?" I said. If he'd never seen it, at least he wouldn't have hated my daddy so.

"The day after Treva died, Dad was just sitting in the sunroom, staring at the empty couch. He read the letter then, and it was like somebody had set off a bomb inside him. He tore into your mama and daddy's bedroom and started throwing Harold's stuff out. He took their wedding photograph off the wall and ripped out the picture and threw it in the stove."

I stared at Aunty Rose, knowing how scared she must have felt seeing Grandpa act that way.

"He started burning your daddy's clothes. Then he got the gun. Mom shoved me out the door and said to run to Uncle Retus's and stay there until she came for me."

I put my hand on Aunty Rose's arm. "Stop," I said, tears running down my face again. I didn't want to think of Grandpa like that.

Aunty Rose swallowed. "I know," she said, choking back her tears. "It was awful. But you were our sunshine. Our only hope. You helped fill the empty place in Dad's heart. That's why he wouldn't let Harold come anywhere near you. He buried the baby off by itself out of spite, and I know he feels sorry about that."

"Sorry enough to make up with Daddy?" I asked, knowing the answer.

Aunty Rose shook her head. "What's done is done," she said. "What's said is said. It would take a miracle to make peace between them after all this time."

I nodded.

We sat there for a while, cross-legged on the floor. I felt as drained as if I'd run up a mountainside.

Finally we put the things back in Grandpa's drawer, trying to make ourselves look innocent.

Chapter 15

Aunty Rose's explanation of what happened didn't help me close the divide between Grandpa and Daddy. Aunty Rose was right. What was said was said, and what was done was done.

Since we'd been back from Oklahoma, Grandpa had been nicer to Daddy, but the rift between them was still about as wide as the Mississippi, and I was getting worn out running back and forth across the bridge.

I tried to settle into school, and Daddy found regular work wiring houses a few miles north of Panther Fork. In early October, he asked me if I wanted to spend a Saturday helping start a job on a big farmhouse on the old toll road.

Saturday morning, as we drove west, we watched pillars of clouds building on the horizon.

"Looks like rain," Daddy said. "Hope the man's attic doesn't leak."

The lunch sack Nana had packed bounced between us on the truck seat. She'd tucked in leftover biscuits and bacon and two pieces of pumpkin pie. I'd added some of the fudge Aunty Rose and I had made the night before.

"Have you forgotten everything I showed you?" Daddy asked, turning in the drive at the two-story brick farmhouse.

"I could fish cable in my sleep," I told him as I helped unload the blowtorch and lantern.

"Good," he replied, putting his hand on my head. He stood watching me, a roll of Romex over one shoulder. "I think I've got a lead on a pretty good place for us to live."

I swallowed, wishing Daddy wasn't looking right into my face.

He took his hand off my head. "Well, you can think about it, Mae Bug."

We worked until about four, coming out into the windy rain that we'd heard lashing the roof all day.

Once we packed our stuff and got on the road, I asked, "Remember that bathtub, Daddy? Wouldn't a warm bath feel good right now?"

I was filthy, and my arm was skinned where I'd lost my footing and fallen against a rafter.

"That place I was telling you about has a nice bathroom," Daddy said. Then he added, "Not that it should make any difference."

"We may be able to just stand in the road and take a shower," I said, pointing to the next thunderhead coming over.

Water stood between the rows of corn stubble in the fields. A web of lightning connected sky and earth for an instant and thunder rumbled.

Daddy watched the storm as we drove into it. "That's got hail in it. See those orange streaks?"

Just then the trees alongside the road bent low and lightning danced around us. The first drops that fell against the windshield were rain. Then little pellets of ice followed, pounding the truck.

Daddy leaned forward, straining to see the road. Hail rolled toward the ditches, which were running full.

"Glad the farmers got their corn in." Daddy yelled to

be heard. "This would ruin their crops. Has Will got all his picked?"

"Except what was down in the bottom," I yelled back.

About that time, the hail stopped. But rain kept pounding on the road faster than it could run off, and I felt water bucking the truck.

We were going right down the middle of the road, lights on, the windshield wipers whipping.

"The door is leaking," I said, scooting over to the middle as the water sprayed my right shoulder.

Daddy didn't spare it a glance. "We better hope we don't meet anybody," he said. "Or one of us is going to get washed out."

We rumbled across the low wooden bridge over Panther Fork Creek. The creek boiled even with the bridge, making little eddies over the planks. Overhead, a railroad trestle crossed the road and the creek at an angle.

The mile to our turnoff seemed to take half a day.

"You sure we haven't missed it, Daddy?" I said, gripping the dash, looking for landmarks.

"I'm not sure of anything," he said, hunched over the steering wheel.

"There!" I said. "There's Andersons' barn."

Daddy slowed and turned. The truck settled in the mud, fishtailing at first. But Daddy kept it out of the ditch.

We were almost home. In about half a mile, Grandpa's barn loomed out of the storm on the right, and I took my first full breath in a long time. When we pulled into the drive, I leaned my head back in the seat.

"You're a good driver, Daddy," I said, feeling like I didn't have a muscle left in my body. "I didn't think we were going to make it."

Daddy stopped the truck behind the house. The rain was letting up some.

"What's a little rain to an old navy man?" he asked. But I saw his hands shaking as he switched off the motor.

Day had turned almost into night, partly because of the thick clouds, partly because it had taken us so long to get home.

I could see Nana against the lamplight inside, watching for us.

"Well, you ready to get wet?" Daddy said.

"Sure. You coming in?" Then I answered my own question. "You better come in."

I could sense Daddy weighing waiting out a storm with

Grandpa against trying to make it on down to Grandmother and Grandfather Clark's without going in the ditch or washing out someplace.

Nana opened the door and made a megaphone with her hands. "Harold," she called. "Come in."

Daddy nodded at me, then we opened our doors and ran for it.

I could tell by the way Nana practically yanked us inside that something was wrong.

"Will hasn't come up from the bottom ground," she said.

Her cold fingers smoothed my wet hair off my forehead.

Aunty Rose came running from the sunroom. "You've got to go look for him, Harold," she said, making hand motions like she was just waiting to turn my daddy around and push him out the door into the storm. "The radio says that west of here, they've had seven inches since—"

"Rose," Nana said, closing her fingers around Aunty Rose's wrist. "Hush."

"Maybe Will just got the tractor stuck, and he's walking out," Nana said to my daddy. "But I'd think he'd be here by now."

"How far back is he?" Daddy asked. Rain ran down his face from his hair.

"About three-quarters of a mile," Nana said. "Which way did you come in?"

"Along the old toll road," Daddy said.

"Then you might have seen him. The bottom ground is just south of the bridge."

Daddy and I glanced at each other, remembering what we had seen.

"Which side of the creek was he working on?" Daddy asked.

"Could be either. He planted on both sides."

Daddy nodded again.

All I could think of was Grandpa wading Panther Fork Creek in the summer and fishing out a water moccasin to show me.

Nana drew me to her side. "You better get out of those wet clothes," she said. "Rose, help Willa Mae find something dry."

How could Grandpa get in real trouble? He'd lived on Panther Fork Creek all his life. He'd be walking in any time now, muddy and mad at getting the tractor stuck but wanting his supper.

"I think I can make it back up the road," Daddy said. "There's nobody's ruts but my own. I'll have a look for Will."

"Rose," Nana repeated, her voice stern and her hand firm on my shoulder this time as she guided me toward Aunty Rose, "take Willa Mae. She needs dry clothes."

Aunty Rose clasped my hand and tugged me to the back of the house. I heard Nana say, "You better take a rope . . . never know . . . hurry. . . ," and Daddy said, ". . . shovel . . . extra lanterns. . . ."

Aunty Rose's teeth were chattering. She nudged me through my bedroom door and started yanking open my drawers like she was mad at me.

A wave of fear washed over me. Could Grandpa really be in trouble?

"You go ahead and get my clothes out," I said, turning to run back to the kitchen. "I need to tell Daddy something."

I slipped out the kitchen door and through the darkness to the truck. Nana and Daddy were coming from the machine shed, each carrying a lantern. I got in the truck and hunkered down on the floor on my side, shutting the door behind me, not worrying that they would hear the noise in the pounding rain.

I curled up and hardly breathed when Daddy opened the door on his side. He turned out the lanterns and set them on the seat inches from my face. The smell of kerosene made my eyes water.

Daddy slammed his door and started the truck. I stayed where I was until he'd driven quite a ways up the road. Then I uncurled, saying, "Daddy, I don't mean to scare you—"

He yelped and jumped so high, I was afraid he'd either tackle me or spin the truck around in the road before he settled back down and I could finish my sentence.

"—but I wanted to come with you to see about Grandpa."

I guess the silence was just because Daddy couldn't find his voice for a while. It didn't last long. Before I could even get the lanterns set on the floor and myself in the seat, he lit into me.

"Did you tell Rose you were coming along?" he asked.

"No, I—"

"Don't you know they'll be worried? What will they think has happened to you?" Daddy shook his head in the darkness, and I could feel his judgment. "I better take you back. I'll turn around up here at the road."

"No, Daddy! Please." I swallowed, sorry that I was causing worry. "Hurry. What if Grandpa is hurt?"

Daddy shook his head again, but at the corner, he went left toward the bridge instead of turning around, and my body went limp with relief.

205

The rain let up for a minute, but thunder pounded in from the west. Great, deep surges of light rolled across the countryside as if giants were looking for something tiny in the landscape.

"Will the lightning get us, Daddy?" I said, suddenly scared not only for Grandpa, but also for us.

"There's nothing we can do about it," Daddy said, his wide-eyed face illuminated in one of the washes of light. "Lightning is like the ocean. It does what it does. It's big."

Daddy hit the brakes and the rear end of the truck waved back and forth as he spun the wheel, trying to keep it under control. A flare of lightning lit the area in front of us. Where a road and a bridge should have been was a swirling mass of water spanned only by the railroad trestle overhead.

"The bridge is out!" Daddy said.

The truck came to a stop, rocked back and forth by eddies. Daddy shifted into reverse as another burs...ng bomb of lightning lit up the creek.

"Did you see that?" Daddy yelled to be heard over the thunder. "Look. Ten o'clock."

He was backing up as fast he could go, hanging out his window, straining to see behind us in the darkness, trying to escape the fingers of water.

Where was ten o'clock? What had Daddy seen? I gripped the dashboard.

"There," Daddy yelled, when he had finally gotten the truck away from the rising creek. He pointed ahead and off to his left. All I saw was pitch darkness beyond the weak beam of our headlights.

"I don't see . . . ," I began. Then the rain eerily stopped its pounding for a minute and the sky lit up like day.

"There," Daddy yelled again, cutting the motor and leaping out of the truck. "Across the water. It's Will's tractor."

On the opposite side of the creek, I glimpsed what he was pointing to. I clapped my hands over my mouth to catch the scream.

In another burst of light I saw the red tractor clearly, flipped over, its front tires up in the air.

Daddy was scrambling to the roof of the truck. I heard the weight of his body overhead. I thought for a minute that he'd lost his nerve and was trying to get away from the rising water that had taken the bridge, then I realized he was getting a better look across the creek. I stepped out, going knee deep in water, hanging on to the door handle.

"Do you see Grandpa?" I cried.

"Wait for the lightning," Daddy said.

Suddenly the lightning was our friend, and I begged it to come, prayed for it to help us.

By the time it surged, I was up on top of the cab too and thought I saw Grandpa pinned under the tractor.

I clutched Daddy's sleeve as the world went black. "How are we going to get across the creek?"

"Only way is the trestle," Daddy said.

"The railroad trestle won't wash out, will it?" I asked, my voice choking.

Daddy scrambled off the roof of the cab, my question lost in a roll of thunder. He reached up for me.

Although the rain and wind were cold, Daddy's body was warm. He lifted me to the ground as easily as if I was a baby.

"Get the lanterns," Daddy said. "And the rope. I'll get . . . ," and his words were cut off by the rain as he waded toward the back of the truck.

He came back with a shovel and his small gray metal toolbox.

Trying to run in the darkness, we sloshed through a flooded bean field. Mud sucked at my shoes, and I stumbled trying to keep up with Daddy.

At the foot of the steep bank that led up to the railroad tracks, Daddy tied one end of the rope around my waist, yanking the slipknot.

"When I get on the tracks, I'll jerk three times on the rope. Then you climb up. I'll be pulling you. You bring the toolbox."

He closed my fingers over the handle.

As he scrambled up the bank, the lanterns over his left shoulder banged against each other. Now and then, the lightning, which was dying down, showed me what was happening. Once I saw Daddy clinging to a scrub bush, which pulled out of the ground, and I heard the sliding sound of his shoes scraping through mud.

"We're coming, Grandpa," I whispered. "Daddy's coming."

Finally a circle of lantern light glowed from the railroad trestle, then another, and I felt the three jerks on my waist.

My hands were slick with sweat and rain as I clung to the rough rope. Brambles grabbed my clothes and tore my skin, and I felt the cold rain washing warm blood down my thigh after Daddy pulled me through a sticker bush.

The lantern glow grew closer, and finally Daddy's hand closed around my wrist and hoisted me onto the tracks.

We seemed to be standing right in the roiling clouds,

and I couldn't breathe. What would happen if a train came along?

Grandpa always said he'd whip me if he ever heard of me setting foot on the tracks. He said a person could get caught, and a train would come along and just slice them in two.

Daddy was coiling the rope and draping it over his shoulder. Wasn't he afraid?

He picked up a lantern and the shovel in one hand and thrust the other lantern and toolbox at me.

My hands went out automatically and took them.

I followed Daddy, watching my footing as we stepped from tie to tie. I tried to go faster, tried to stay close, but my legs trembled so much, I was afraid I'd fall.

"What if a train comes along, Daddy?" I gasped, hoping he'd hear me and turn around.

He stopped, looking behind us, and I caught up with him. I put the lantern and toolbox in the same hand and grabbed his coat sleeve.

"It won't take long to cross the creek," he said, not answering my question. "We're going out over the water now."

Fighting dizziness, I looked down at the wide, swirling creek below us.

Daddy clasped my hand. "It'll be kind of like walking a cross beam," he said. "Think you can do it?"

I nodded, then realized he couldn't see me in the darkness. "I think so," I whispered.

"I'm going to call your grandfather," Daddy said. "I'm going to call out to him just to let him know we're coming."

Daddy swung his lantern in front of him, and I did the same, copying his moves.

"Will!" Daddy yelled. "Will Shannon!"

I tried to sort out the sounds that came back to us. My lantern made a squeaking sound as it swung, and Daddy motioned me to quit. The creek rushed below us.

Please answer, Grandpa, I prayed. *Please.*

Daddy set down his lantern and cupped his hands to his mouth. "Will!" he shouted again. "Can you hear us?"

I listened so hard, I heard Daddy's leather belt creaking as he took breaths.

Finally a weak "Yo" came back.

I started shaking, and Daddy hugged me to his side. Then he took my hand again and we moved out on the tracks, over the water forty feet below. I saw it swirling between the ties.

"Don't look down," Daddy said, his voice tight.

I clung to his hand and began counting my steps. I'd

go ten steps. Then I'd see if I could work up the courage to go ten more. My knees shook so much, I doubted I could make my feet go where they needed to. But I just kept counting.

I went to ten, then twenty. When I got close to a hundred, Daddy said, "We're almost there."

"How come we brought your toolbox, Daddy?" I said, making myself talk to keep my mind off the last few steps.

"You never know what we're going to find," Daddy said. "We may need tools."

As soon as we were over the water, he stopped.

"Will!" he called.

Grandpa's weak "Yo" came back.

"We're on your side of the creek now. Up on the tracks," Daddy yelled, holding his hands to his mouth. "Can you see our lanterns?"

We swung them in front of us again.

After a long time, Grandpa called, "I see them." His voice sounded weak.

"Watch our lanterns," Daddy hollered. "When we're even with you, call out." Daddy's voice sounded strong over the sound of the wind and water, but up close and underneath, I could hear him fighting to catch his breath.

We went along the tracks at a trot, things rattling in

Daddy's toolbox, my heart lighter and my feet more sure of themselves.

After a while, Daddy stopped.

"Are we even with you, Will?"

"Just about," Grandpa said, his voice closer. "Another fifty feet."

Going down the embankment was faster than going up. I skidded ahead of Daddy, digging my heels into the mud. The toolbox slipped from my hands and I winced at the sound of rattling metal rolling away into the blackness. Rocks scraped my hands and bottom, but it didn't matter. I could fly if I had to, walk on water, lift the tractor off Grandpa single-handedly.

"Over here," Grandpa said, his voice very close.

I could make out the bulk of the upside-down tractor. Up close, it even smelled dangerous, the reek of fuel oil floating on water.

"Here," Grandpa said. "My foot's caught, Harold. Who's with you?"

"Willa Mae," Daddy said, shining his lantern over Grandpa.

I stepped into the light so Grandpa could see me. Only the top part of him showed. The rest of his body was hidden under the mass of the tractor.

Grandpa's face shone a sickly bluish white. He repeated my name in a puzzled voice as if he was thinking about who I might be. Then his head jerked with recognition. "Willa Mae," he said, reaching out his left hand.

I set down my lantern and squatted beside him, clasping his hand between mine.

"How long you been here, Will?" Daddy asked, bending to look closely at Grandpa's face.

"I don't know," Grandpa said, his voice slow. "A long time."

He shut his eyes, almost like he was falling asleep, and his grasp on my hands loosened.

"Grandpa! Grandpa!" I shook his hand.

Grandpa opened his eyes, and I nearly fainted with relief. I squeezed his hand, rubbing it.

Daddy was moving his lantern around, sizing up the situation.

Grandpa's eyes closed again, but he kept a grip on my hand. "I been watching the water come up, Willa Mae," he said. "It was a sight."

The rising creek was only about four feet away from Grandpa's head. "I supposed the creek was going to get me. Still might, if your daddy can't get me loose."

I made a sound of denial deep in my throat as Daddy spoke from the darkness. "I'll get you loose, Will."

His voice soft, Daddy told me to find out if Grandpa was hurt anyplace except what was under the tractor.

I ran my hands over Grandpa's icy head and face. Had Grandpa hit his head on a stone?

As I slipped my hands under his head, his eyes came open. "Look," he said. "There's the Big Dipper."

Grandpa was seeing things. The sky was thick with clouds.

"Look, Willa Mae," he insisted. He was coated in a slurry of mud from struggling to get loose, but his blue eyes glowed in his streaked face, focused for the first time. "Look up there."

I looked just to indulge him. Sure enough, the clouds had parted, leaving a gap so we could see the Dipper.

"It's beautiful," I said, my voice singing. "I never did see anything so beautiful."

I sat back on my heels. "Where are you hurt, Grandpa?" I asked. I hadn't felt any wounds or broken places. "Can you move everything?"

"Everything but my left foot," he said.

He rolled his head to stare at the water, and he shuddered. The rain had stopped, but the creek was still rising.

I concentrated on the hungry, gnawing edge of the creek, willing it back. If I wished hard enough, it would leave my grandpa alone.

"That smokestack saved you, Will," Daddy said, starting to dig around Grandpa's legs.

"It held the weight of the tractor off me."

The smokestack, on the nose of the tractor, had hit sandstone when the tractor rolled over. It kept the heavy machine propped up just enough to spare Grandpa's life.

In the silence of the wind dropping for a minute, I heard the creek still chewing and Daddy breathing hard as he threw out shovel after shovel full of mud. Grandpa waited in breathless silence, his eyes closed again, his hands twining between mine as if we were washing up for a meal.

"Try pulling your foot, Will," Daddy said, standing back and leaning on the shovel handle. He pushed his wet hair out of his eyes with muddy fingers.

Grandpa's hands tightened around mine and I felt his body go taut.

"Grandpa," I said, straining with him. "Pull."

I saw his left knee rise with the effort.

Daddy dug some more, panting. Was the water only about three feet away now?

"Try again," Daddy ordered, panic bubbling in his voice.

Grandpa stared into the stars and shuddered with the effort of trying to pull his left leg out. "You pull on it, Willa Mae," he said with a groan. "I think the rain washed my strength away."

"Come on, Will," Daddy said, throwing his shovel back and leaning his weight into the tractor.

"Tell me if it hurts you," I said, trembling at the thought of somehow making things worse.

I straddled Grandpa, hooked my hands under his knee, and pulled back. I heard him suck air between his teeth. "Keep pulling," he said.

Suddenly the tractor moved and a cry escaped from Daddy before he knocked me away and grabbed Grandpa under the shoulders and heaved, pulling him free.

Both men lay in the mud, entwined. The tractor tilted a little, then settled.

While Daddy followed the edges of the creek south to the Penningtons' place, I stayed with Grandpa, talking to him, rubbing his hands, and curling my body around his to keep him warm. After a long time, I heard a tractor coming over the hill to get us.

Chapter 16

The week before Christmas, Doc Simmons stopped by and sawed the cast off Grandpa's foot. Grandpa's impatience with casts and crutches blazed in his eyes and he threatened to throw the crutches in the woodstove. But the doctor said if Grandpa didn't want to be crippled for life, he better keep the weight off his leg for a while longer.

Grandpa grumbled, sick to death of listening to the radio and reading the Bible and visiting with the neighbors who still dropped by. But what had been a torrent of friends right after the tractor accident was now down to a trickle—mainly just the preacher and Uncle Retus's family. Everybody could see that the farm was well in hand, thanks to my daddy. The pump didn't squeak anymore,

Old Jerse got milked morning and night, and things around the place worked as well as they could considering they were tended by a son-in-law, which people seemed to now remember my daddy was.

He went off most mornings to work wiring somebody's house or farm, but he came back every night and did Grandpa's chores: milking, tending the pigs, and helping Nana get the henhouse ready for winter. When Daddy went across the road to turn out the sheep, I went along. My lamb had grown almost as big as her mother and would eat out of my hand.

After the chores were done, Daddy came in and washed up for supper. I'd see him sitting across the table from me in the lamplight, and it felt good.

And the best part of all was that after supper, and after Daddy had talked to Grandpa about a sore place on one of the sheep's sides—or whatever other problem he'd noticed—he'd go upstairs to bed. Daddy stayed in the east bedroom, under the eaves, where he and Mama used to sleep. That room was right over mine, and I could hear him moving around. I wondered if he was remembering Mama, and if the memories made him happy or sad.

Memories work both ways, I guess. Back in November, on a windy night that I'd figured out later was the anniversary of Mama's death, Grandpa had hoisted himself from his chair by the stove and onto his crutches. He'd disappeared into his and Nana's bedroom and came back after a while with a picture in his hand.

"Treva sure was pretty, wasn't she?" he'd said.

Then he'd wiped the silver-framed picture with the sleeve of his flannel shirt and set it on the sideboard.

Lowering himself back into the chair, he'd sat gazing at the dancing flame that showed through the stove door.

In the quiet, we'd listened to little sparks of wood popping.

Daddy'd cleared his throat after a while. "Yes, sir. She sure was."

That night in bed, I'd cried myself to sleep, but only because I was glad.

As the weeks worked up to Christmas, I got in the habit of stopping by Mama's picture. Some days she seemed to be looking right at me, and for the first time in a long time, I thought she might be taking an active interest in my life.

"I'm learning to cook, Mama," I whispered one day when I was alone in the room. "Nana has showed me how to make fried potatoes and biscuits. We're going to try a pie crust on Saturday."

Meantime Daddy was scrambling to get Nana and Grandpa's house wired by Christmas Eve because Nana had her heart set on Christmas tree lights.

In the evenings, we'd hear him up in the attic singing, then he'd break off and yell for me and I'd scramble through the opening in the ceiling of the cedar closet to give him a hand with the blowtorch or whatever he needed.

And Nana was pushing to get the living-room walls covered with the red-velvet patterned paper she'd bought with her egg money. So the week before Christmas, Aunty Rose and I took turns slathering the strips of paper with thick, nose-stinging paste. Nana hung each strip herself, counting on Grandpa to tell her if the pattern was running straight.

With all this going on, the days till Christmas flew by. December twenty-third was Grandmother Clark's birthday, so Daddy and I went down that night to take her a pretty box of lady's dusting powder.

She'd put a roast in the oven, and apples baking with raisins and cinnamon perfumed the house. Aunt Belle had made a spice cake with special seven-minute frosting that swirled in peaks over the cake.

Grandfather Clark brought out his dandelion wine for the occasion, and this time I had a sip.

"It's good," I said, testing the taste on my lips.

Later, after we'd eaten our fill and sung "Happy Birthday" to Grandmother Clark and looked at the card Uncle Lesley sent her from Oklahoma, we went out into the starry night to get in the truck. The tip of my nose turned cold. The truck's heater didn't work very well, and Daddy carried a blanket for me to wrap up in. I pulled it around me and watched for who had Christmas tree lights sparkling through their front windows.

"There's the Bradshaws'," I said. "Look, Daddy. They've got a lighted angel on top of their tree."

The Marshalls, down on the corner, didn't have a lighted angel, but their tree lights were shaped like candles.

At Uncle Retus's house, the living room was dark except for the blaze of the Christmas tree.

"Won't Nana be proud," I said, "when we plug in the lights tomorrow?"

"Sure hope it happens," Daddy said. "And it will if the inspector gets out."

The inspector didn't come the next morning, though Daddy stayed home to wait for him. About noon, Aunty Rose and I went to town to do last-minute Christmas shopping but, most of all, to stop by Morton's Hardware Store and pick up the lights that Nana had finally decided on.

Snow started to fall about the time we turned north on the highway, and fat, wet flakes kept right on tumbling down. By the time we came out of the hardware store with a sack full of lights, the streets were slick and Aunty Rose slid through a stop sign on the square.

"We better get home," she said.

"Just one more stop," I begged. "I want to get Marilee and Mattie something."

They'd given me a locket as a Christmas present. Marilee had fitted a tiny picture of herself into one side of the locket, and Mattie had done the same on the other.

And although Aunty Rose didn't know it, Petey Tyler had slipped me a small package when we were putting on our coats after the Christmas program at school last Wednesday night. I'd hidden the present in my pocket and had not opened it until I was alone in my bedroom with the door closed. Inside the folded and refolded red-and-white-striped paper was a brass bookmark with a heart engraved on it.

I wasn't going to tell anybody about the present—not that I didn't appreciate it. Mostly, I guess, I liked that Petey had paid enough attention to know how much I enjoyed reading. But if Aunty Rose knew he'd given me a gift, she'd tease me day and night.

The sparkling blue ear bobs from Charles Michael winked in and out of the waves of her hair as she parked the Packard in front of Herbert's Drugstore.

"Let's hurry," she said.

In the window, I saw a display of Evening in Paris perfume.

"You stay here," I commanded her. "And keep your eyes shut."

She grumbled, but I could tell she was giggling inside. And I knew she'd peek and try to find out what I was buying her.

Inside the front door, pine boughs scented the air. A lady with a tightly curled glossy hairdo helped me choose a small bottle of Evening in Paris for Aunty Rose and a matching set of tortoiseshell hair barrettes for Marilee and Mattie. I had exactly twenty-seven cents left from the money Daddy had given me for Christmas shopping.

On the way home, we had to drive slowly. The snow had stopped, but the roads still glistened treacherously.

The winter sky blazed with sunset by the time we drove past Panther Fork Church.

"Let's stop here a while," I said.

Aunty Rose parked outside the gate, and we walked up

the path, which had become just an indentation in the snow.

"Lonnie Dale's mama put a wreath on his grave," Aunty Rose said, pointing.

The wreath, hung with red Christmas balls, had been lavishly decorated by snow.

"It's pretty," I said. "I wish I'd brought Mama something."

Aunty Rose took a deep breath, then let it out, making her breath billow in the cold.

"I sure do miss her," she said.

I nodded.

Our footsteps squeaked in the snow. A cardinal flew from one cedar tree to another, and I caught a whiff of Aunty Rose's perfume. I knew she'd like her Christmas present tomorrow morning.

She drifted off to pet the preacher's beagle, who'd ambled over from the parsonage, and for a minute I had Mama to myself.

Mama's angel wore a pom-pom of snow on her head, giving her a festive look that made me smile inside.

It's working out okay, Mama, I said, looking into the soft winter twilight. *Daddy's being home and all. We're all settled down now.*

A jay landed on the branches of the redbud that grew by Mama's grave. The jay's weight shook snow down, which showered on my face. Somehow it made me think of Mama laughing. I knelt and drew a butterfly in the snow, and that was when I saw the little bouquet of juniper berries tied with string.

Who had been here before me? Daddy? Grandpa?

What difference did it make? We all missed Mama.

Hoping Aunty Rose didn't follow, I drifted over to the little grave by the fence. It cast a blue shadow on the snow.

I bent down to touch the letters.

Baby Clark was happy in heaven with Mama, no matter where his body lay, but because the rest of my family was right here at Panther Fork instead of in heaven, I wrote in the snow, *"We love you, little brother."*

At home, everybody was standing around the fireplace in the living room, champing for Aunty Rose and me to get back. The wiring inspector had come while we were gone and hooked up the meter.

But no lights had been turned on yet. They were waiting for the Christmas tree decorations.

Nana beamed as she studied the picture on the box of brightly colored candles bubbling with light.

"Hurry," she said, "before it gets too dark."

So in the darkening room lit by the glow from the fireplace, we strung the Christmas lights, Daddy climbing up on a chair to do the high ones and Grandpa giving advice from the wall where he leaned with his crutches.

"Are you ready to plug them in, Mae?" Daddy finally said, stepping back.

"Wait," Aunty Rose said. "Let's sing 'Silent Night.'"

So we began. But because we weren't singers, we just smiled and moved our lips now and then while Daddy sang out in his strong tenor.

Silent night, holy night,
All is calm, all is bright.

When he was done, Nana leaned down and plugged in the Christmas lights, and we all clapped. Aunty Rose and I hugged each other, and Nana beamed her thanks to Grandpa and my daddy.

Later, while Nana was working on supper, I bundled up and went outside. I could hear Daddy still singing in the barn about the Christmas child.

Jacky ran up to me silently in the snow and prodded my hand with his wet nose.

I petted him, my strokes making static electricity crackle in his cold fur.

"I know what one of my packages is under the tree," I told Jacky. "It's buckskin gloves from Daddy."

Daddy didn't sing about the gypsy Davy much anymore, I guess because we weren't gypsies. But I'd seen the leather gloves in the window of The Mammoth Department Store. They were small enough to fit my hands and made of the softest tan leather.

"Spanish leather," I'd said, trying them on that day in the store. "Just like the song says."

Not that I needed them for wandering. For now, our traveling days were over. For now, we were all happy exactly where we were.

About the Author

Sharelle Byars Moranville remembers the miracle of electricity: ice cubes, ice cream, bright lights at the flick of a switch, and especially her father scrambling to get her grandparents' farmhouse wired before Christmas so there would be lights on the tree. Ms. Moranville grew up in deep country darkness. "My grandpa could show me the splash of the Milky Way on any clear night—so the changes rural electrification brought were profound," says the author. Several years ago, Ms. Moranville discovered a batch of family letters from 1945 that opened up a world of memories, inspiring her to write Willa Mae's story.

A professor of writing and literature, Ms. Moranville lives in West Des Moines, Iowa, with her family. This is her first novel for young readers.